ONE FINE VOICE

By

Rebecca Langston-George

HISTORIUM PRESS U.S.A.

ONE FINE VOICE

Copyright © 2026 by
Rebecca Langston-George

This is a work of fiction inspired by historical events. Names, characters, places, and incidents are products of the author's imagination or are used fictitiously. While certain historical elements are based on true events, the narrative has been fictionalized to explore themes creatively and is not a literal account of history.

HARDCOVER ISBN: 978-1-964700-60-1
PAPERBACK ISBN: 978-1-964700-59-5
EBOOK ISBN: 978-1-964700-58-8

HISTORIUM PRESS
U.S.A.

For my husband,
Reverend Robert George

CONTENTS

CHAPTER 1

The End

One word. Two little syllables. My brain might've known that was all it was, but my heart . . . oh, my hot, empty, aching heart knew what came after that word. A full-stop, no-going-back, period on the sentence that meant the end of our chapter in Meadow Springs.

"Goodbye."

Dorothy said the word first, her arms wrapped around me as we stood behind the Model T where Mama and Daddy waited inside with the windows rolled down, chatting with the neighbors who had gathered around the car. They'd all said their back-thumping, tight-hugging goodbyes already.

"It'll be okay," Dorothy said. "Think of it as starting a new adventure. Like choosing a . . ." Her voice broke, "a new book off the library shelf."

I nodded, even though I knew finding new friends would be far more complicated than pulling a book off the shelf. And, consarn it all, I liked the friend—or book, I already had!

Still, I knew what was expected of me, so I pasted a weak smile on my tear-streaked face and promised, "I'll write. It'll be just like always."

A little lie, like a dab of honey, helps you swallow unsavory things easier, like the word goodbye and its ending punctuation.

"Esther," Daddy called. "It's time to go."

I didn't want to go.

I wanted to stay and even though it was the first day of summer, I wanted to go to Meadow Springs School and sit next to Dorothy Hoover just like I, Esther Hopkins, had done ever since my first day of school. Why, the alphabet itself had pre-ordained that we would be best friends for life!

But no one ever listened to what I wanted. My voice didn't seem to matter.

When I finally climbed into the backseat, I pushed against my father's battered old Army footlocker trying to make more room. But it didn't budge. Just like my father. This move was all his doing. A promise he had made nearly five years ago in a trench in the Western Front. My father, the farmer, promised God he'd serve him and become a minister if he lived through the Great War in Europe. It had taken him several years and a lot of studying, but my father was making good on his promise.

Daddy started the car. Mama leaned out the open window to hug Dorothy's mother. As Daddy pulled the car through the gate and onto the road, Mama and I turned to wave through the back window until we couldn't see our friends any longer. Only Daddy looked forward, straight ahead, driving to Grayson, Indiana, and a new life. A new job waited for him there where he'd be ordained as the new Baptist minister.

What did the road ahead hold for me?

CHAPTER 2

A Frozen Lamb

Daddy knelt in front of the altar two days later on June 3, 1923 to be ordained by the Regional Minister for the Indiana Baptist Fellowship, Reverend Dewhurst. The old, bald-headed man laid his gnarled hands on my daddy's head and prayed God's guidance down on him something powerful.

Oh, mercy, you could feel the spirit surging through the room toward Reverend Dewhurst's voice. The congregation waved their funeral home cardboard fans back and forth in the humid June heat, urging the Holy Spirit forward like a great rushing wind at Pentecost. It flew up the aisle, right by me, fluttering my ginger bangs, and soared smack dab into Reverend Daddy as he was anointed the new minister at First Baptist Church of Grayson, Indiana.

Reverend Daddy rose up off his knees till he reached all five feet, eleven-and-a-half inches of himself, or six feet, by Daddy's rounding. Even though Daddy, Mama, and I were strangers to the congregation, having just moved to town yesterday, the congregation nodded and "Amen-ed" their new minister all the way down from the stage and back to his seat between Mama and me, just like we were old friends. Even though I was still sore at my father about the move, I couldn't help but be proud of him today—a day he'd worked toward for so long. I reached for his hand and gave it a squeeze. Reverend Dewhurst lifted his palms, motioning everyone to their feet to sing.

The pianist plunked out "The Old Rugged Cross." Since I do not tell lies in or about church, I will say that "plunked" was being mighty charitable on my part. I leaned forward and looked to the left to catch Mama's eye. She kept her eyes right straight ahead, but I could see the smile crinkle around her blue eyes. She'd find a way to get her hands on that piano, but quick. Music coursed through Mama's very blood. Before Daddy became a preacher, every one of his kin had been a farmer, Daddy included. As he tugged at his stiff white collar and creaked with every movement in his shiny black shoes, I remembered how his overalls and farm boots agreed with him better. When it comes to music, I take after Mama's side. Daddy says I sing like a songbird. But, to my father's eternal consternation, I dress like the farming side of his family that we'd just left behind in Meadow Springs.

The pianist hit a wrong note in the chorus, causing Mama to wince, just as the church's back doors wheezed open. A girl with a big blue hair bow in the next pew turned to look at me. Our eyes locked. Then she turned toward the doors behind us. I followed her gaze. That's when I first saw them.

White robed men wearing pointed hoods paraded up the center aisle. They marched together in pairs until they reached the altar where my daddy had just knelt; then half went left and half went right, forming a line across the front of the church. Their faces were masked save for the cut-out eye holes. Those sunken, shadowed holes all stared right at me, it seemed, pulling my eyes toward them, locking me in their dark gaze, paralyzing me with their murky eyes.

I tried to sing. I knew every song in the hymnal by heart. But just like the white masks staring at me I didn't have a working mouth. I tried to read the words in the hymnal, but I couldn't tear my eyes away from those blank stares. The one thing in my body that worked was my memory. It jabbed a stick in a deep muddy pool of my mind that usually only bubbled up in my nightmares.

Four years ago, a winter's day. A crust of ice crunched underfoot as I walked with my uncle to his barn. A lamb had gotten loose and had frozen to death near the fence, its white wool stiff with sparkling ice crystals. A black crow was perched atop its head, a dark berry dangling from its beak. The crow flew away, and I saw that the lamb's eyes had been picked out. Its cold, empty eye sockets stared through me, and I screamed.

I felt that same urge to scream right then and run clear down the street away from our new church. I even turned my head toward the back door, but something stopped me. The girl—the one with the big blue bow—she was singing--like she probably did every Sunday. I blinked. I turned my head the other way. Daddy sang along in his strong tenor. Blink. Reverend Dewhurst held his hymnal high and sang toward the ceiling. The pianist plunked on. Mama was the only other one that looked confused. Everyone around us was acting as if nothing unusual was happening, like masked robed men marching into church was perfectly normal. Was this normal for Grayson, Indiana?

I took a deep breath. Forced my eyes to focus high above the pointy heads, at the warm sunlight streaming through the stained-glass window above the altar. It painted a kaleidoscope of muted colors on the church's east wall. I leaned toward the safety of my father and rested my head against his arm. Felt the starched smoothness of his sleeve and smelled the clean pine scent of his shaving soap.

As the last piano note hung in the air, one of the robed men took a step forward. He handed a smiling Reverend Dewhurst a bulging envelope. From behind his mask came a deep, gravelly voice. "A gift for the Baptist Fellowship in honor of your new minister from your brothers in the cross."

Reverend Dewhurst placed his bent, arthritic fingers on the man's white-robed shoulders and drew him so close his bald head made a dimple in the other man's pointed hood. "Thank you, brothers. May God bless this donation and use it to advance his righteous work."

The crowd "Amen-ed" and "Halleluh-ed" the masked men as they shuffled in their long white robes back down the aisle toward the door. One of them, shorter and rounder than the others, turned his head to cough as he passed my pew, and I caught a strong whiff of peppermint. For a moment, his watery eyes, so pale gray they were nearly colorless, fixed me in their hollow stare.

After the men exited through the creaky doors, Reverend Dewhurst ended the service with some announcements. I realized Blue Bow was watching me as I clutched my father like a toddler. Embarrassed, I shifted my weight so I was no longer leaning against him. He wasn't mine for long anyway, as people crowded around us after the service. Their words were friendly, welcoming us, promising to invite us to dinner. But their eyes told a different story, taking stock of our clothes, our hair, our fingernails, and judging our worth. I felt like a bolt of cloth being measured for a dress.

"How do you do?" It took me a second to realize Blue Bow had stuck a white-gloved hand out toward me. I shook it and the beaded bag on the crook of her arm bounced up and down. "My name is Iris Westin. My father is one of the deacons. He tells me you're Esther." I nodded. Unlike my father, I did not have the gift of gab, especially with new people. She waited.

I determined to make more of an effort. "Yes. I'm Esther."

She waited.

"Hopkins," I added. "Esther Hopkins. And you're Iris, you say." As though that helped.

"Well." Iris sniffed, her eyes darting down to my scuffed shoes and back up to my rough bare hands before smiling. "I'm sure we'll be good friends, Es."

I smiled back, knowing neither one of us believed that. She was a delicate store-bought china doll, and I was just a handful of rough, dried cornhusks, twisted and bent to resemble a doll. Still, the girl was well-spoken; had to hand that to her.

"Outside, everyone, please proceed outside," Reverend Dewhurst waved the crowd toward the door.

I followed behind my parents and joined the congregation on the church's front lawn. We all gathered around a big white sign lying face down on the grass.

A man walked toward my father, introduced himself as Deacon Holland, and handed Daddy a mallet. "We thought you'd like to do the honors, Reverend," he said.

Another man helped Deacon Holland pick up the sign and fit its legs into holes in the ground. Daddy rolled up his sleeves and swung the mallet over and over again, pounding the legs deep into the hard brown earth. In bold blue letters, the sign read, "Grayson Baptist Church, Reverend Paul Hopkins, Pastor."

When it was secure, the congregation cheered. People smiled and clapped Daddy on the back. Reverend Dewhurst shook his hand and whispered, "You'll do fine here. Grayson's a good, God-fearing, all-American town." Mama hugged Daddy. I smiled, but as I looked around, I couldn't help but wonder. Where had the masked men gone?

CHAPTER 3

A SUNSET SANCTUARY

You don't have to be the minister's daughter to know there are ten commandments. Mostly, they're things you can't do, like thou shalt not murder. The fourth commandment comes in handy once a week for not doing things: "Keep the Sabbath day holy. Six days shalt thou labor and the seventh is a day of rest." But here it was, after church on the Sabbath, a day of rest afforded me by God himself via some stone-chiseled tablets handed to Moses, and my mama insisted we scrub the kitchen in our new house and unpack all the barrels of dishes. She claimed there was an exception for people who just moved, especially people who just moved into a parsonage next door to the church.

I gave my father the side eye when he remained silent despite Mama's plan to ruin a perfectly good summer day. I knew better than to say out loud that he, of all people, should have known the ten commandments. But, truth was, Reverend Daddy was a little loose with the fourth commandment but clung tight to number five: "honor your father and mother". He returned my side eye and threw in a raised eyebrow to boot, before pointing at the barrels of dishes. It was just like him to overrule my plan to sit on my rump and read. He grabbed a handful of crackers and cheese before leaving to meet with the deacons next door.

Mama and I dusted all the pantry shelves, washed down the walls and counters, scrubbed the kitchen floors and unpacked the dishes. My knees grew red and chafed from scouring the floor with a brush, and the scarf I'd tied around my hair was covered with bits of packing excelsior. My back ached from reaching into the barrel of dishes.

When Mama pronounced the kitchen in order, it was nearly 7:00 in the evening.

There was still time, though, in my own way, to keep this day holy because the most consecrated part of any day is sunset. I climbed the stairs to my room and stood at the window to look out. The rosy light painted the sky in sherbet hues behind the church steeple as evening wrapped its summer shawl around the shoulders of our back yard. The last quiet wisps of the day were still mine.

Removing my shoes, I put my new treasure in the pocket of my apron and climbed out the window and into the waiting arms of the oak tree beside my bedroom. As I snuggled into the cleft between branch and trunk I breathed in its earthy odor. I'd recognized it as a kindred spirit the moment I saw it yesterday. When I realized I could climb into it from my bedroom window, I thought God himself had arranged it for me, a peace offering to replace all I'd left behind in Meadow Springs, and that's when I decided to forgive God for uprooting my family from our home and sending us here. We weren't even yet, me and God. By my accounting, he still owed me, but the tree paid a large chunk of the debt.

I pulled the treasure from my pocket. *The Baptist Hymnal*, its scarlet cover stamped in gold, *First Baptist Church, Grayson, Indiana.* It wasn't exactly mine, but it wasn't exactly anyone else's either. Hymnals were only used on Sunday mornings. Come Sunday I'd sit in the pew where it belonged, and I didn't need it then. I could already sing all the songs. Outside of Sunday mornings—that's when I needed the words, the poems set to music. I didn't know when I'd get to a library again for a book. When I did, it just wouldn't be the same without Dorothy by my side. I needed books now more than ever, since I didn't have her to talk to. But with a book, even a song book, I could escape. I could climb up this tree to read, to think on things and ponder, to fill me up with music and beautiful words. Mostly, I needed a book to keep me company, to keep me from remembering all I'd left behind.

I thumbed through the gilt-edged pages and found some words, true as any scripture, to whisper to the fading pink and gold sunset as it slipped away into the night. "Oh, Lord, my God, when I in awesome wonder, consider all the worlds thy hands have made. . . thy power throughout the universe displayed."

As the darkness grew, the electric lights inside the church blazed brighter like candles set to light the way. Then they went out. Daddy's meeting was over. From the church yard next door I could hear the deacons' goodbyes, a trill of laughter, and a car engine rumble to life. The sound of their departure splintered the night's sacred stillness, swept the last remnants of daylight into the night's dark dustbin.

Daddy would be home soon. I tied my head scarf around the hymnal and tucked it into a hollow spot where a limb had broken off. Maybe my father wouldn't mind me borrowing the hymnal. Maybe he'd understand that this tree was a sanctuary to me as much as the building next door was to him, but truth was, sometimes Daddy and I didn't see eye to eye on right and wrong. Best keep it to myself. What he didn't know wouldn't hurt him.

As I came downstairs I could see the light in his office. His back was turned to me as he pulled books from a carton behind his desk. It was odd seeing him dressed in his suit at night. Odder still to have an office in our home. Though it had shelves of books, Daddy's study books were off-limits. I didn't mind much. Judging from the titles on the spines, they seemed to hold lots of dry religious history. Still, the room felt a little mysterious. Daddy had made this room all his, and even before he had an office, he'd long retreated into books as an escape from remembrances of war. I understood his need to have a place all his own, kind of like my tree. Still, it felt odd, having a room in our new home where I knew I wasn't really welcome.

"Why do you have that?" I asked, pointing to a trowel looking out of place lying atop his desk.

Daddy turned, *Spurgeon's Commentary on Great Chapters of the Bible* in his right hand. He placed the book on the shelf beside his desk and picked up the small trowel. It was rough and worn, dotted with rust, but free of dirt. "It's to remind me of where I came from."

I stood silently, surprised my father wanted to remember he came from a potato farm. I motioned to one of the chairs in front of his desk. "Can I sit down?"

He nodded and sat at his desk. It felt strange and formal, having a desk between us.

"Who were those men in church today? The ones in the masks?"

He lifted his glasses and rubbed his right eye. "They call themselves the Ku Klux Klan. Deacon Westin says they're a club, a social group. He tells me we have half a dozen members in our church. All good upstanding patriots, he says."

Daddy tapped the newspaper on his desk. "Now, I've heard reports about some old branches down south stirring bigotry and hatred after the Civil War, but that was a long time ago, more than 50 years, but not here in Indiana. . . And war . . . war does strange things to people. So much hatred. So much violence." Daddy's eyes drifted away. He stared at the evening darkness that filled the window.

After two minutes of watching my father stare silently at the dark window, I stood to leave him alone with his thoughts. But that roused him, and he turned his eyes back to me. I wanted to keep talking and get his mind away from war, so I asked "They don't look like a club. What do they do?"

"Well," Daddy paused to think, his face troubled. "I hear they raise money to build hospitals and help widows. They support the local Protestant churches, giving donations—like they gave to our church today. In fact, every member has to belong to a local church, and," he straightened the blotter on his desk, his voice wavering as he continued "I'm told the club promotes high moral standards in the community. That's a good thing. Can't protest a group doing good things."

"They do good works with masks over their faces?" The minute I said it, I wished I could take the sarcasm back.

Daddy frowned for a moment, looked away at the window, then turned back and spoke softly as though he were telling his books, not his daughter. "It's the only open church I could find, Esther. The only place I could follow God's call and serve the Lord. Maybe we can be of service here."

"But, why do they dress like that?"

"Club people do odd things," Daddy said, his voice suddenly full of life. "Your Uncle Jack is a Mason, remember? He wears that ridiculous fez. Tassel spins around every time he turns his head." Daddy laughed nervously.

I had a feeling the masked men were nothing like my gentle Uncle Jack who'd trudge miles through the snow to find a lost sheep, but I let it go. Daddy turned back to his books, turned his back to me. Conversation over.

CHAPTER 4

COFFEE CAKE AND CATHOLICS

It was a simple request. I knew from experience it's best to get straight to the point in prayer and not waste God's time. He is a busy man. Or spirit. Or something. The point is, I made it clear. Eight words. "God, please send me a new best friend." Actually, it was nine if you count the "Amen," but who counts the "Amen"?

The tree, or MY tree, as I'd come to think of it, was a good place to talk to God. Back nestled against the trunk, bare feet dangling in the cool air, I listened just in case he cared to answer. Green leaves rustled, whispering secrets to one another, a fat bee hummed to herself as she passed, and a trio of robins sang in the leafy green choir loft above me. I wished Dorothy were here. She would have appreciated this tree. It had been four days since I'd said goodbye to her. Four days since I climbed into the back of our Model T and watched Meadow Springs disappear in the rear view window, and my best friend along with it. Four days, and still no sign of a friend here in Grayson, despite my very clear prayer.

I looked up through the leaves at a patch of blue sky. "Don't forget," I told God.

As if in reply, the back door slammed shut below me. Apparently the Almighty didn't take kindly to reminders.

"Are you sure you want another coop?" I heard my father ask in the yard below me. "There's not nearly the room here. It'll be right next to the church."

"Now, Paul. You promised, and I want it just like the last one." Mama handed him a ball of string and paced out where she wanted it.

I quietly drew my dangling feet up on the branch where the leaves would cover them. Eavesdropping was sinful. But unplanned eavesdropping was just lucky.

My parents were marking the coop's perimeter with stakes and string when a voice called over the gate. "You back there, Reverend?"

Before Daddy could answer, Mr. Westin barged into the yard. "Ah, yes, they're here!" He called over his shoulder. "Margaret and I wanted to pay a little social call to welcome you." His wife followed with Iris right behind.

Mr. Westin added, "And of course, Iris couldn't wait to see her new little friend again." He patted her on the back and she flinched, as though the thought of being my friend was distasteful. Just as well. She wasn't the kind of friend I had in mind either. I glanced toward heaven to drive this point home.

Mrs. Westin held up a cloth-covered plate. "Cinnamon coffee cake."

"And mighty tasty!" Mr. Westin added. "Why, Margaret's coffee cake won the blue ribbon at the last two county fairs. Isn't that right, honey?"

Mrs. Westin fixed him in a frosty stare. "Four years, actually."

Mr. Westin took off his straw hat to fan himself. "Well now," he waved his hat toward the string, "What are you folks planning?"

"Tilly wants a chicken coop," Reverend Daddy answered, wiping his hands on his overalls.

"A chicken coop? Next to the church?" Mrs. Westin wrinkled her nose and looked pointedly at her husband.

Mama took the plate from Mrs. Westin's hands and gave her a steely gaze, but Daddy's eyes darted between the stakes and the church, a wisp of worry clouding his face.

"Yes . . . well . . ." Mr. Westin patted his wife's arm before addressing Mama. "Good to see you're settling in."

Mama turned to Mrs. Westin. "Shall we go inside for some of your prize-winning coffee cake?"

Daddy led them toward the kitchen door. Over his shoulder he said to Iris, "I'll call Esther downstairs for you."

I needed to skee-daddle back through the window quick. But little miss good-manners allowed everyone ahead of her through the door. Then she turned, looked up at me with her big, green eyes and sighed before going into the kitchen.

As I scrambled through the window and buckled my scuffed brown shoes onto my bare feet, I wondered what Iris Westin was up to. I put my oldest apron over the frayed, worn dress I had chosen for cleaning today. I'd look like I was the housemaid, but if our visitors wanted to see us in fancy dress, they should have mentioned they'd be coming to call.

Mama served the cake and coffee on her best blue willow china service in the parlor. Mr. Westin balanced his delicate cup and saucer on his right knee and accepted seconds and thirds on the cake. With his mouth busy, Mrs. Westin kept up the chatting, informing Daddy the church foyer needed repainting. "Tell the man at the hardware store you want porcelain eggshell---not white. Too glaring, don't you agree Reverend Hopkins?"

Daddy agreed, but changed the topic before Mrs. Westin got it in her head he was the church's handyman. "I'm sure our guests would enjoy some music." He nodded at Mama and me. "Tilly and Esther, would you mind?"

Back in Meadow Springs, our parlor was full-to-bursting every Friday night with laughing, singing neighbors who'd come to hear Mama tickle the ivories. When she played, it was like the music found its way into the hungry parts of your soul. Daddy said she poured her heart into the piano. But really, Mama coaxed that piano into pouring out its own heart. She could make it soothe your deepest sorrows and shoo your worries clean out the door. Mama had loved our farm back in Meadow Springs, had loved the view out the window looking over the sheep pasture as she played the piano. The chickens and sheep had perked their heads up at the sound. Aunts, uncles and cousins always gathered around when Mama played. When Daddy returned home from the war a shadow of the man he'd been before the war, Mama played even more, sending her melody and her voice clear to Heaven.

Without knowing it, Mama had apparently prayed and sang God's call down to Daddy to become a preacher, much to our surprise. But church was the only place Daddy found that soothed his soul after the Great War. When Daddy decided to become a preacher everyone back home said if a church committee was smart, they'd hire Daddy just to get Mama's piano playing free in the bargain.

I wasn't much in the mood to sing for the Westins, whose friendship so far chafed like new shoes against a blister, but I was proud to showcase my Mama's talent. I stood beside her as she settled on the piano bench and began playing "Come Thou Fount of Every Blessing."

Mr. Westin got swept away right off, smiling and tapping his foot to the music. I'd have bet he would have sung along if his wife hadn't been beside him. The longer we performed, the more eager Mrs. Westin looked, sitting on the edge of her chair like a cat waiting to pounce on a mouse. Iris, though, looked nervous. She had a big handful of her yellow, lacy dress twisted in her right fist.

When we finished, Mr. Westin applauded and patted me on the back as I walked back to my seat. "That's one fine voice you have there!" He turned to Daddy. "Reverend, I heard tell your wife was talented, but I had no idea it ran in the family. Mrs. Hopkins, do you sing as well?"

Mama shook her head. "That's Esther's department. I just play. My father taught me." She stroked one fingertip gently over the worn gold lettering above the ebony keyboard. "He built pianos."

"Lloyd?" Mrs. Westin jumped from her seat and stood next to Mama to read the trademark. "Do you mean to tell me you're related to the piano craftsmen the Lloyds?" she asked incredulously.

Mama's face beamed. "My father was Obadiah Lloyd."

Mrs. Westin slid next to her on the piano bench, cozy as a mewing kitten. "Do you give lessons?"

"You want to learn to play, Mrs. Westin?" Mama didn't look pleased at the thought of having Mrs. Westin sit on her piano bench every week for lessons. "I suppose we could . . ."

Mrs. Westin cut her off with an impatient wave. "Not for me. For Iris, of course."

Everyone turned to look at Iris, pale and staring at the wrinkled fabric in her fist. Daddy looked at me and coughed, his eyes darting between me and Iris. I knew that look: his call to Christian action. What was I supposed to do? The Bible talked about helping widows and orphans, but didn't cover comforting spoiled rich girls forced to take piano lessons.

I held in a sigh. "Iris, shall we go on the porch to get some air?"

Without taking her eyes off her pale dress, Iris walked to the front door and waited for me to open it as Mama and Mrs. Westin discussed practice times. Outside, I plunked myself on a porch step while Iris dusted her side of the step before lowering her delicate backside.

"Don't you want to play the piano?" I asked. "Mama is an excellent teacher."

"What I want," Iris said, lifting her eyes to stare at the church next door, "never matters."

Thinking of Daddy and his end to our conversation, I felt a little pang of recognition. Debating whether to feel sorry for her, I decided instead on diversion. Pulling a stub of chalk from my apron pocket, I said, "Let's play hopscotch."

Iris frowned, but I didn't care if she was too high and mighty to toss a rock and hop around. At least it was something to do besides watch her mope.

I chalked the squares on the asphalt road. The straight white lines, sharp and new against the black pavement, reminded me of doing sums with Dorothy on the schoolroom blackboard in Meadow Springs.

I plucked two smooth stones from the flower bed and tossed one to Iris. She rolled her eyes and sighed the sigh that rightfully belonged to me before tossing the stone just outside the first square.

"That's too bad," I said, "Better luck next time."

"What are you talking about?" she asked, kicking the gray stone inside the square with her toe. She jumped over the stone and through the other squares before hopping back to the beginning.

"That's cheating!" I protested.

Iris shrugged. "So? At least it's not eavesdropping."

Any sympathy I'd felt for her shrunk to a small cold stone and dropped to the pit of my stomach. There she stood, hands on the yellow chiffon sash around her hips, daring me to do something. To say something.

But, I didn't. Iris wasn't worth the trouble. She was the worst kind of cheater—one who cheats even when the stakes are low. No point in wasting words on her. Had I been in church, I might have admitted the uncomfortable truth about me and words in the presence of bullies and cheats. Instead, I shrugged and threw my stone.

As I jumped I saw a dark-haired, olive-skinned girl on the other side of the street. She paused, leaned against a tree and watched us.

"Hey," I called. "You want to join us?"

The girl hesitated, then walked over. "Do you live in the church house?" she asked.

"Yep." I pointed to the new church sign next door. "Reverend Paul Hopkins—that's my father. I'm Esther."

The dark-haired girl bobbed her head in greeting. "I'm Anne-Marie Lombardi."

"Pleased to meet you." I knelt down and dug another stone from the flower bed. "Do you know Iris already?" I brushed the dirt from the stone. "You two in the same class?"

Anne-Marie nodded toward Iris before throwing her stone smack-dab in the middle of the first square like a hopscotch champion.

"Es," Iris said, glancing at the parsonage window where her father's back was visible through the glass. "I don't care to play any longer. "I . . . we . . . we have to go inside now." She dropped her rock with a tiny thwump and climbed the porch steps, turning at the top to face me. "Now, Es. We need to go in now."

When I didn't move, Iris went inside without me. I turned to Anne-Marie. "Something I should know about between you two?"

Anne-Marie crossed her arms over her chest, her brown hair swinging across her shoulder. "I don't suppose she cares much for me."

"Why is that? Have you been mean to her?"

Anne-Marie laughed. "A lot you know, new girl. My family aren't the mean ones in town."

Questions tumbled in my head, but none came out as I picked at a loose thread on the pocket of my apron. What did she mean?

"Look," Anne-Marie said. "we still playing or do you suddenly have to go inside now that I'm here, too?"

I glanced up at the window and shook my head. Nimble as a jack rabbit, Anne-Marie Lombardi hopped through the chalk squares then challenged me. "Ever try to hop it backwards?" She asked. "Go ahead, I dare you."

We hopped backwards and laughed and fell on our backsides until the front door opened a few minutes later. The Westins stepped on the porch, followed by Mama and Daddy.

"I best go," Anne-Marie said. "My grandpa runs the feed store. Come by and see me soon, Esther."

As I waved goodbye and climbed the steps to the front porch, Mrs. Westin nodded towards Anne-Marie's back and whispered three syllables loudly to Mama from behind one white-gloved hand, "CATH-O-LIC."

I opened my mouth, but words always failed in times like these, so I stood there, facing Mrs. Westin with my mouth slack as a broken Christmas nutcracker. Iris shook her head a fraction of an inch, warning me to stop without knowing I didn't have it in me to even begin.

"We must be going," Mr. Westin said. He patted me on the shoulder. "Young lady," he asked "how would you like to sing on Independence Day? My club's putting on our annual Patriotism in the Park picnic and parade. There'll be food, fireworks and," he leaned closer to me and winked one pale gray eye, "a pretty young newcomer singing a solo. If you say yes, that is."

Excited, I turned to Reverend Daddy. "May I? Please?"

Daddy laughed. "I doubt wild horses could stop you once you've put your mind to something." He pulled me toward him in a hug.

I caught my breath. A rare hug from Daddy made me feel even more eager. I turned back to Mr. Westin. "Thank you, Deacon Westin. I'd love to."

"Excellent!" Mr. Westin exclaimed. "Now, I don't suppose you two girls would like a sweet?" He winked at me, then Iris, as he drew a small white paper bag from his pocket. He shook a little red and white ball into each of our upturned palms.

Smiling, I popped the peppermint into my mouth.

CHAPTER 5

SIGNS ALL AROUND

Mama likes to say "The early bird catches the worm." I say the early bird catches people off guard, so I swung my feet out of my cozy bed the next morning just as dawn showed its fresh scrubbed, pink face through my window. Downstairs, I lit the gas stove and put the copper tea kettle on to boil.

I heard Mama's feet on the stairs before the cast iron skillet had even sizzled.

"You're up early," she said.

"You've been so busy unpacking I thought I'd cook and give you a rest." I laid bacon in the skillet and smiled at her.

I pulled the egg basket from the ice box. "Too bad we have to make do with store bought eggs. I sure miss your fresh ones." I paused to whisk the eggs to a yellow froth. "I heard there's a feed store in town. We could go ask about chickens there."

Mama stirred a spoonful of honey in her tea. "I don't know what you've got up your sleeve," she paused to sip, then smiled. "But, I would welcome a stroll into town."

The smell of bacon brought Daddy downstairs as I was slicing store-bought white bread for the toaster. Mama piled bacon and scrambled eggs on his plate. "Good eggs, dear," he said. "Light and fluffy."

Mama nodded toward me. "Esther made breakfast this morning, and you needn't compliment my eggs. You know we haven't arranged for hens yet. They're from the grocer."

Daddy raised a strip of crisp bacon to me in salute then sniffed. "Is something burning?

I ran to the smoking toaster. "Darn it!" I yanked the metal levers toward me to pull the scorched bread away from the glowing electrified coils.

"Language!" Reverend Daddy reminded, that familiar scowl on his face.

"You have to watch it carefully and remember to turn the bread," Mama chided gently. "Otherwise it's wasteful." She poured herself more tea. "Can you do your chores and be ready for town by nine?" I nodded.

Daddy leaned over to brush burned toast crumbs off my apron, "Wear some clothes suitable for town. First impressions count, you know," he said. Mama and I exchanged doubtful looks. "I don't want people thinking the new minister dresses his daughter from the charity bin." I snapped off a bite of bacon instead of telling Reverend Daddy he worried too much about appearances for his own good. We'd only been here a few days, but he acted like we didn't quite belong, like we had to prove ourselves. Considering the fact that following God's call was what Daddy said he wanted, it sure was wearing him out already.

The town square was only two blocks away. Freshly swept sidewalks lined the square's perimeter. In the center, like a glittering emerald set in a sterling silver ring, lay the town's park. Giant oak trees crowned with summer's leafy majesty dotted the lawn. Twenty carved wooden benches faced stone steps leading to the stage shaded by a white pergola. Lush green vines and delicate fuchsia blossoms cascaded down its side like spring bridal bouquets. I caught my breath realizing I'd sing in that fairy tale setting in two weeks. Oh, won't it be wonderful! I closed my eyes to imagine myself up on that stage. But, before I had time to savor the sin of vanity, Mama took my elbow and steered me down the street.

We paused to peer in the window of Holland's Sweets and Tobacco. The name was stenciled in curly black script under the window's green and white awning. An ivory card fastened inside the glass pane read "100% American." The sign perplexed me, but the tall glass confectionary jars of licorice, lemon drops and taffy begged for my attention. Alongside them stood tins of rolling tobacco, plugs of chew and cigar boxes. Mr. Holland saw my nose pressed against the glass and waved us in.

By the door we passed the most striking cigar advertisement I'd ever seen. The face of the carved wooden Indian statue was so realistic I thought he might suddenly tell us hello. His intricately chiseled feather headdress made him taller than the door he guarded. He stood atop a large, worn wooden block that read "Chew Virgin Leaf." One hand held a bunch of carved tobacco leaves. The other shielded his eyes as though searching for someone or something in the distance. I wondered if he was looking for the Native Americans who'd been driven out of Indiana, the very state named for them.

Mr. Holland, smelling strongly of tobacco, came from behind the counter to greet us. "I see you met the chief. You ladies come downtown to do some shopping? Maybe candy shopping?" He winked at me.

"Shopping, yes," Mama answered. "Candy, no."

"Then perhaps candy sampling? My welcome to town treat, Miss Esther." He turned to Mama. "With your permission, of course."

Mama smiled. "I don't suppose one candy will spoil Esther's lunch. You are very kind, Mr. Holland."

Mr. Holland waved at the glass jars. "What'll it be young lady? Lemon drop? Licorice? Maple stick? Maybe a nice peppermint? They're long-lasting and leave your breath crisp as a winter breeze."

I hoped he wasn't hinting my breath needed attention, but I pointed to the licorice whips. "May I have a licorice, please?"

Mr. Holland brought me the jar so I could select one.

"Thank you, sir," I said.

"Please give my best to Mrs. Holland," Mama added. "We'll see you Sunday."

The bell over the shop door bade us a cheerful, tinkling goodbye. But something in the druggist's window next door caught my eye.

"There's another of those signs, Mama. A hundred percent American. What do you suppose that means?"

She shrugged. "I don't know." We walked a few more steps and saw another sign at the barber shop. Mama said, "Maybe it's an advertisement for a product, like the tobacco sign on the base of the wooden Indian."

I stopped in front of a door labeled Truman T. Anderson, Esq., Attorney at Law and pointed to the 100% sign tacked to it. "Attorneys don't sell any products. So that can't be it."

Mama just shrugged again and frowned as we passed three more businesses with 100% American signs before we reached a store window painted with the words "Lombardi Feed." I tugged at Mama's sleeve. "Look. No sign here."

Inside an old man with a luxurious waxed gray mustache bowed politely to Mama and smiled. "Hello, hello. How can I help you? I am Lombardi. I take care of you."

"We just moved here and I need to purchase some items. I'm Tilly Hopkins."

"Ah, Signora Hopkins. Your husband is the Baptist priest, no? And this is your daughter?" He smiled at me. "You met our Anne-Marie, eh?"

"Nipotina!" he called over his shoulder. "You have company."

Anne-Marie emerged from the thick maroon curtains that cordoned off the back room as Mama continued with Mr. Lombardi. "I want to set up a chicken coop. Can you help me?"

"Si! Yes, yes, Signora Hopkins. Certainly. How many chickens do you keep?"

"Well, I still need to get the chickens, but I usually keep fifteen or so."

Mr. Lombardi smiled. "Perhaps I can assist you. I do not keep too many chickens here anymore. My business has not been so good lately and . . ." His voice trailed off as Anne-Marie turned to look at him. "Ah, but no matter. I have seven good chickens out back and I can get more. Permit me to show you."

He led Mama out back as Anne-Marie perched atop a pile of oat bags and motioned for me to join her. I pulled the red licorice whip from my pocket. "Want half?" I asked, tearing it in two.

Anne-Marie frowned. "Where did you get it?"

"Mr. Holland gave it to me."

"I figured. No, thank you."

Since it had taken some foresight on my part to choose a candy that's easily shared, not to mention the remarkable amount of restraint I had shown in eating neither my half nor hers already, I was, to be honest, annoyed. Especially given the fact that now I couldn't eat either half right in front of her. It must have shown on my face since she added, "Look, you're new here, so you don't know how things are. It's nice of you to offer, but Mr. Holland doesn't like my family. We don't trade with him. It would be like . . . well, it'd be like betraying my mother and grandparents."

Before I could ask any questions Mama and Mr. Lombardi were back. Looking very pleased, he led Mama to the cash register and rang up her sale. "Seven chickens, four bales of straw, and twenty pound of feed. I can deliver that today, if you like, Signora."

"Wonderful!" Mama counted out the money from her purse. She looked happier than I'd seen her since we'd left Meadow Springs, and I wondered if Mama had been sending up prayers of her own for friends of the feathered sort. "But let's say the day after tomorrow so my husband can finish building the coop."

"Nonno, may I go with you when you deliver it?" Anne-Marie asked.

"Si." He held up one long calloused finger. "If your madre agrees." He winked at me as Anne-Marie raced behind the counter and through the curtains. She came out followed by a tall dark-haired woman with wire-rimmed glasses framing stern brown eyes.

"This is Mrs. Hopkins and my friend Esther, who I told you about. And this is my mother, Civilla Lombardi." She gestured toward her mother. "May I go visit them when Nonno delivers their feed?"

Mrs. Lombardi shook Mama's hand. "I suppose you can go. That is, if it's alright by Mrs. Hopkins. She may not want company underfoot until she's settled in her new house." Mama assured her it would be fine. "What grade will you be in when school begins, Esther?"

"Sixth," I said.

Before I could ask, Anne-Marie said, "Same as me. And you just met your teacher. Can you believe I'll have to do what she says at school as well as at home, now?" She crossed her arms and pretended to look put out, but I could tell Anne-Marie was proud of her mother.

"Well, we'll have to see," Mrs. Lombardi eyed her father-in-law, whose expression turned sour.

"We see. Yes. We will see if that school board comes to their senses." He turned toward Mama and me. "Now, I have a gift for you, my good customers." His dour expression lifted as he handed Mama and I each a small cardboard calendar, the size of his palm, from a stack beside the cash register. It was navy blue with the store's name in gilt lettering forming a horseshoe around the months.

We thanked him and I pointed to the date two days away. "See you then, Anne-Marie!"

A few doors down we almost collided with Mr. Westin coming out of his grocery store. He had a white sign in his window, too. "Mrs. Hopkins. How nice. Do come inside."

"Thank you, but we're not buying groceries today. We were just buying feed and a few chickens from Mr. Lombardi."

"Oh." He continued to stand, blocking our way. "Mrs. Hopkins. If I may. Perhaps—for the future—I can recommend a, uh, more suitable feed store. Mr. Cafferty, from my lodge, runs a small feed establishment over in Muncie. He could deliver anything you want. Chickens, feed, anything you need. Very trustworthy, Cafferty."

Mama's head cocked a bit to the side as it always did when she was confused. "A more suitable store? I'm not sure what you mean, Deacon. I'm sure your man Cafferty is indeed a fine businessman, but Lombardi is right here locally."

Mr. Westin coughed, but Mama continued. "And Esther's made friends with his granddaughter, you see."

He coughed again. "Well, now, it's a question of loyalty, isn't it? As a fine upstanding American you want your dollars to help patriotic countrymen like yourself, don't you? Not lining the pockets of foreigners or papists. That's why we've got to make sure we trade with others who share our views, not foreigners."

Mama pursed her lips and met his gaze square on like she was gathering her words, words I suspected my father wouldn't appreciate. I felt my cheeks burning hot as I managed to blurt, "We have to go." There was so much more I wanted to say, but the words lay tangled and mute in my dry throat as I steered Mama into the street to go around him. But he put his arm out and followed us.

"Well, of course, it's no matter. Being new in town you had no idea. And, well . . . seven chickens." He waved off the idea. "I'll introduce Reverend Hopkins to some of the other businessmen in my lodge. I'll ask Cafferty to stop by the parsonage on his next trip here." He removed his straw hat and fanned himself. "Why, after just a few Sunday dinners you'll need more chickens anyway, now won't you?"

Mama turned pale, but he blustered on, clapping her on the shoulder before adding, "You know, we should get together for supper, soon. Why, I bet you're a dab hand at frying up a chicken, seeing as how you raise them. Yes, indeed! Nothing like a fried chicken leg, crisp and golden, piping hot out of the pan!"

Mama grabbed my elbow and I thought she might faint at the idea of frying her own chickens.

Mr. Westin, however, didn't look at all fazed by the thought of ingesting a chicken of questionable loyalty.

CHAPTER 6

CIRCLE OR CROSS

Some days start with sunshine and bird song. Other days start with oatmeal. Lumpy, gray and gluey, mine was also cold because I'd overslept. Adding raisins, sugar and cream almost made me forget it was horse feed.

I forced down a bite as the doorbell rang. Mama turned to look at the grandfather clock. "Must have gotten the time mixed up. She's a half-hour early."

Before I could ask, Mama dried her hands on her dish towel and said, "Iris. Piano lessons."

With the back of my spoon, I smashed a raisin against the side of my bowl. Mama returned with a basket and Anne-Marie behind her. I was so surprised my hand slipped, shooting a raisin two feet above my head. Anne-Marie laughed. "Bet you can't do that again!"

"She better not," Mama said, placing five delicately speckled brown eggs on the counter. "Don't waste food, Esther." But Mama's eyes twinkled, so I knew she wasn't scolding, just Mama-ing.

"Nonno says they're yours since you bought the hens."

"Thank you for bringing them, dear, and please pass on my thanks." Mama motioned Anne-Marie to sit. "Would you like some oatmeal?"

"I've eaten, thank you. He asked if ten o'clock tomorrow would be convenient for your delivery."

"Let me ask Rev. Hopkins if the coop will be ready." When Mama walked away, Anne-Marie tossed a raisin high above her head and caught it on the tip of her pink tongue.

"Catch this," I said, flicking a raisin at her chin.

Even over our giggling, we could hear Mama and Daddy's voices getting loud and contrary in the office before their conversation dropped to a low, steady insect hum.

Mama returned wearing the triumphant look of a wasp that had delivered a well-deserved sting and told Anne-Marie ten o'clock tomorrow would be fine. Without asking me if I was finished, she picked up my oatmeal bowl and took it to the sink where she attacked it with a scrub brush.

I motioned for Anne-Marie to follow me to the front porch. We sat on the top step where the sun hadn't yet creeped.

"Your mama reminds me of my mother," she said. "She's got some vinegar to her."

We sat for several minutes before I got up the nerve to ask what had been on my mind. "It seemed like your mother was uncertain whether she'd teach or not." I paused to find the right words. "And the school board?" I could hear my voice trailing off.

"She's a good teacher. A fair teacher. Writes lessons every night and grades papers. She works hard." Anne-Marie sniffed. "It's those hundred-percenters. They run the school board, the businesses, everything. We're Catholic, and they say she'll obey the Pope instead of the school board, so they're holding a meeting to decide . . ." She paused to pick up a granite pebble from the step. "To decide if my mama is fit to teach." She threw it with all her might across the street, hitting a maple tree with a tiny thwunk. "She's gotta teach, see. Grandfather's store isn't doing well."

I sucked my breath in as Anne-Marie went on. "Nonno and Nonna, they came on a boat from Italy—they weren't born here." The meaning of those 100% American cards I'd seen everywhere except Lombardi's hit me like a baseball bat to the head.

I touched her arm. "What about your father? Can't he--"

She interrupted. "My father died of influenza when I was ten months old. That's why we live with my grandparents."

Even though I hardly knew Anne-Marie and her family, I knew what hard times can do to you. Back in Meadow Springs, Mama had attended seminars at the library to learn how to conserve food and do our part for the war effort. I remembered picking piles of green beans for Mama to boil, can, and share with neighbors.

And I loathed, hated and absolutely abominated unfairness and people who acted better than everyone else. My heart hurt for Anne-Marie. But what could I do? As we sat there silently I made a decision. I linked my arm through hers. "When is the meeting?"

Anne-Marie wiped her glistening eyes with her blue sleeve. "It's six o'clock next Thursday, June 21st at the school auditorium. But my mother will show them. She'll give them an earful."

I nodded. "I'll come too."

Anne-Marie looked so surprised you'd think I'd flicked a raisin clear up her nostril. "You'd do that for me, new girl?"

I nodded. "Next Thursday at six. Just save me a seat."

"Well," Anne-Marie hesitated. "There won't be any seats . . . not for us, at least. Just meet me at the auditorium's back door. Don't use the front entrance. And, don't let anyone see you."

"Huh?" I asked. "Why the back door?

A pair of white-stockinged legs appeared at the bottom of the stairs. Iris, wearing a yellow bow and a smirk, had arrived for her lesson as punctual as the morning school bell. "You're going to sneak in the back, aren't you?" She shook her finger at me. "Don't do it, Es. Children aren't allowed at school board meetings. She'll get in trouble and so will you." Iris paused for dramatic effect. "If I decide to tell my father on you."

Licking her lips, Anne-Marie said icily. "As I was saying, there won't be any seats for us because children aren't allowed at school board meetings. So meet me by the back door where we'll wait for my mother, who might just be Iris's teacher next year." She rose, climbed down the stairs, and stood, her tan nose an inch from Iris's pale one, before continuing. "With all the power your father has in this town, it's a shame he can't buy you one single friend."

Color creeped up Iris's neck and bloomed across her cheeks. "Excuse me. I'm late for my piano lesson." She jerked her thumb, motioning for me to move and let her pass. Then, purse thumping against her silk and lace side, she marched up the front steps where Mama answered her knock.

Anne-Marie bolted toward the street. "I'll understand if you can't make it that Thursday." Her voice was cool, her brown eyes focused elsewhere. "Watch out for her," she added over her shoulder.

I trudged through the parlor and up the stairs feeling Iris's eyes on my back as she pounded through the piano scales. "Rhythm," Mama reminded, tapping one finger in time with the metronome atop the piano.

As I pulled off my shoes, a shimmer on the wall caught my eye. A faint glint from the gold embossed horseshoe on my calendar winked as a beam of sunlight illuminated it. Fishing the chalk from my apron pocket, I circled Thursday, June 21. I wouldn't let Anne-Marie down. But it was July 4 I couldn't take my eyes off. I held the chalk over the little gold 4, watching it flicker then fade as the sun filtered through the tree beside the window. Circle it, or cross it out?

CHAPTER 7

A PATTERN

The music should have been a clue. I'd seen two movies at the Meadow Springs Cinematic Palace and knew the Wurlitzer organist set the tone for what was coming on the screen. Light, upbeat tinkling music meant a funny show; slow, deep thundering keys signaled you were in for something suspenseful. So I should have been prepared when the harsh, erratic pounding of piano scales downstairs stopped and the villain appeared framed in my doorway.

"Your mother gave me permission to come up," Iris announced, then frowned. "What are you doing sitting in a tree again?"

I held up *Treasure Island* so she could see it through the window. "Reading," I said. "Won't do you any good to tell your father. My parents already know I'm literate."

She pursed her thin, pink lips like she'd just sucked a sour lemon drop from Holland's store as she glanced around. "Are you going to invite me in your room?"

I held the book up again. "Why? I'm not even in my room."

Even from my tree I could hear her exaggerated sigh as she entered and stood beside the window. "My mother asked me to invite you and your mother to tea this afternoon at two o'clock. She has a pattern for the choir robe you'll need for Independence Day."

I nodded, knowing I had no choice in the matter, and turned back to my book as Iris left.

Over lunch, my father once again preached the "suitable clothes" sermon when he heard where Mama and I were headed. Apparently, he didn't want anyone to mistake us for the patched-clothed, dirt-streaked hands-in-the-ground farm family we'd always been. He had to play the part of a minister, a minister suitable for a city like Grayson. So we had to put up with his nerves and play our part too, even if it meant putting up with nasty people and not really being ourselves. So, I had to change into a scratchy Sunday dress before leaving for tea and torture. As I tossed my ratty apron on the bed, my chalk fell from the pocket and rolled across the floor. Picking it up I pondered the Fourth of July once more. Circle or cross out? I wanted to sing on that stage in the park. I deserved to sing on that stage. Yet, thinking about it set off a hum in my head, like an approaching swarm of yellow jackets on the horizon. I wanted that choir robe pattern and I didn't. Chalk in hand, I looked up at the calendar again. But in its place was a bare nail with a navy blue shred dangling from it.

Mama's adherence to Reverend Daddy's clothing sermon went as far as removing her apron and donning her yellow straw hat with three sunflowers and a brim so wide it hadn't been fashionable for several summers. On her arm hung a small wicker basket with a jar of homemade peach preserves and a handful of white daisies from our backyard.

I could tell which house on Maple Street belonged to the Westins without evening looking at the address. It was painted pale yellow with white gingerbread trim decorating every corner and edge. Shirred lacy poufs decorated every window, reminding me of the lace on Iris's dresses.

Mrs. Westin showed us into the parlor where she had laid out tea, lemonade and tiny cakes the size of a half-dollar, iced in pale pink frosting with sugared violets on top. They were a blue-ribbon contender if I'd ever seen one—a real feast for the eyes. Despite the tenth commandment, I coveted my neighbor's confections something fierce.

Our hostess poured, then offered each of us the glass cake stand. The violet atop my cake smelled faintly of perfume. Mummified in sugar crystals, it was brittle and sweet on my tongue. It tasted like plain sugar, tasty, but less special than I had hoped.

After Mama and I oohed and awed appropriately at the fancy treats, Mrs. Westin handed Mama the pattern envelope. "Tell our girl in dry goods I sent you. She'll know the materials you need."

Mama thanked her, but Mrs. Westin waved it off airily. "It's no trouble. We must all do our part to help the new minister and his family." She touched Mama's arm and leaned closer. "I imagine it must be so difficult to make do . . ." She lowered her voice to a whisper, "on a minister's salary." She leaned back as Mama's eyes went wide. "So naturally, when I finished Iris's robe, she's reciting the Preamble to the Constitution, you know, well, I knew it was my Christian duty to share the pattern with you." She turned to Iris. "Go put on your robe so Mrs. Hopkins can see what it looks like finished, dear." After Iris disappeared up the stairs she continued, "How is my little pianist doing?"

Mama, sat up straighter on the Westin's gold brocade couch. "Just as well as can be expected. Which reminds me, we should settle your bill for the first month." Mrs. Westin blinked several times at the indelicate subject, but Mama was blunt as a butter knife. "As you say, so difficult to make ends meet."

Mama tucked the coins inside her hatband as Iris reappeared at the foot of the stairs in a starched white cotton robe that reached her shins. It had long full sleeves and zipped up the front. It was similar to a baptism robe but had a white cord knotted around the middle for a belt.

When Iris turned to go back upstairs I excused myself and followed. Her room looked much like I expected, pink, lacy, frilly and extraordinarily neat. As Iris zipped herself free of the robe, I looked at the pastel drawings on her wall. Arranged in sets of four like window panes, two on top and two below, divided with lengths of pink ribbon, each picture showed the same animal from different views: front, right, left and from a distance. There were five sets in all: monarch butterfly, frog on a lily pad, ladybug, owl, and dragonfly.

"These are beautiful," I said, meaning it despite my distaste for Iris. "Did you draw them?"

She smiled, her eyes sparking with interest, probably the first real smile I'd ever seen on her face. "Yes, I'm working on a crow at my desk."

I walked toward the black chalked picture pinned to an easel by her desk, but instead of reaching for it I grabbed the beaded white bag beside it and dumped the contents on her desk.

"How dare you!" Iris roared as I fished my calendar from a pile of torn notes, creased valentines, ribbons and Sunday school buttons.

"No. How dare you," I shook my calendar at her. "You stole this from me." Next I held up the valentine showing a dancing long-legged bee. *To my best friend Ida. You're the bee's knees! Lillian.*

Iris grabbed the valentine and shoved it back in her bag as I picked up a ribbon stenciled *Abner Greenway, Top Speller, 1922.*

"Give that here," Iris grabbed the ribbon from me. "That ribbon belongs to me."

"I believe it belongs to Abner Greenway," I said before the meaning of her words sunk in. "You came in second, I bet."

Iris's cheeks flushed. I pushed the pile of stolen trinkets toward her, each one a false imitation of friendship or accomplishment. "Why'd you steal from me?"

"You should stay away from her and that feed store. Like I told you, she'll only get you in trouble."

"Trouble?" My mouth went dry as my courage ran out. I willed my finger not to tremble as I pointed at the spelling ribbon and licked my lips. I managed to whisper, "Like when people tell on each other?"

CHAPTER 8

A ROBIN

Taking a walk is a good way to clear your mind. As I walked home with the pattern stowed in Mama's basket on the crook of my arm, I tried to scrub my mind of the image of Iris's face, pink and blotchy, and scared. I wasn't proud of threatening to dose her with her own medicine. Wasn't angry with her either. Guess I felt kind of sorry for her being so jealous of people that she stole from them. I wondered what Iris thought as she clutched that purse full of schoolroom plunder close. Mama once told me people sometimes do mean things to get attention, even to get friends. Seems like the best way to get rid of friends, if you ask me.

A scraggly orange tabby ran past with something brown in its mouth. Something wriggling to get free. Oh goodness, a bird! That cat was going to eat it! I took off after it, chasing it down the street and around the corner into a neighborhood I'd never seen, shabbier than the rest of town, with a dirt path and ramshackle unpainted rough lean-to houses on either side. The cat paused to drop the struggling animal from its mouth long enough to place an orange paw over it and get a better grip with its teeth. The robin flapped one wing for dear life. I lurched for it but the cat was too fast, racing with its prize up Lincoln Street. Behind me I heard Mama calling for me to stop, but that robin needed me.

I followed that orange tail right through a line of laundry hung to dry and ran smack dab into a Black boy a few years younger than me clutching a tub of wet sheets. Wooden clothes pegs hung from his suspender strap. The cat stopped and dropped the bird at the boy's feet, holding it with one rough, scraggly paw as though he was presenting the boy a Christmas present.

"That's my bird." I yelled. "Make your cat let go!"

The boy dropped the metal wash tub and stooped to scratch the tabby's neck. "Cheddar, what've you got there? Let it go." He picked the cat up and the freed robin flapped one wing while the other drooped lifelessly. A tall, thin woman with curly wisps of hair escaping from a bun atop her head, rose from scrubbing at her sudsy metal washboard and walked over.

"What are you doin' here, Miss?" She asked.

Mama caught up, out of breath and hat askew. "Please pardon my daughter for barging through your wash," Mama said. She straightened her hat and extended her hand. "I'm Tilly Hopkins. This is my daughter Esther. We're new here in town."

I picked up the bird as the woman looked Mama over and carefully dried her hand on her faded candy-striped apron before hesitantly taking her hand. "I'm Sophronia. This here's my oldest, Samuel." She nodded over her shoulder at the wee baby tied to her back. "Young one's John." As she let Mama's hand go she added, "Is your man the new Baptist minister?" Mama nodded. "I did the washing for the one afore him, Reverend Smithfield. You in need of a washer woman?"

As Mama and Sophronia talked, I emptied our basket, placed the bird inside and tied Mama's handkerchief over the top. He didn't like it much, flapping and chirping shrilly, but at least he was safe.

The boy watched, clutching the cat tightly against him. "You ain't gonna hurt Cheddar, are you?"

"Why would I want to hurt your mean old cat? Just keep him away from my bird."

He relaxed and released Cheddar. It sniffed the hem of my dress, looked up at my basket, then sauntered slowly away, holding its skinny tail up high, the tip crooked at a right angle, before jumping into a battered red wagon near the washboard.

"Samuel, get that furry beast out of my laundry!" Sophronia called.

Samuel picked the scruffy, thin cat up once more and cradled it. "How's that bird your pet?" He asked.

He had a point. One I was pretty sure would occur to my mother at any moment, not to mention my father. "It's not exactly mine, but it's hurt, and since it's not exactly anyone else's either, I'm going to help it."

He grinned and stroked Cheddar's paw. Apparently we had something in common.

Mama looked at the yellow bird beak poking out of her basket and sighed. "It won't be able to forage for food. It'll need regular feeding until its well enough to fly. You sure you're up to the task?" I nodded.

"Can we go to the library and see if they have some books about birds?" I asked Mama. The library wouldn't be the same without Dorothy, but I had to start somewhere. Mama hesitated a moment, then smiled.

As we turned to go, Samuel said, "Esther, you forgot something." He released the cat and bent to pick up the pattern where I'd dropped it. His hand hovered over it, frozen. When he handed it to me his eyes went wide and blank, his mouth slack with surprise, like he'd just seen a monster. His startled expression followed me home.

CHAPTER 9

DIGGING UP WORMS

The trouble with broken things isn't that they're difficult to mend or no longer useful. The trouble with broken things is they can break other things like your heart and make you long for the time when things were whole. When Daddy came home from the war, I could see in his eyes, in the distance between us, something inside him was broken. When Dorothy accidentally broke the lever on my mechanical bank three years ago, I didn't get angry at the little iron dog that refused to jump through the clown's hoop with my penny. I got angry at Dorothy and nearly let that broken bank break apart our friendship.

A broken wing was no way to start a friendship with a bird. I loved my little feathered friend immediately and tried to let it know by holding its tiny feathered body close and humming sweet music to it. Even though I'd lined its basket with soft scraps of beige fabric from Mama's sewing basket and disinfected the puncture marks on its left wing with hydrogen peroxide, its black eyes followed me warily wherever I moved. Its butter-yellow beak pointing an accusing finger at me. I hadn't reckoned on it blaming me for what happened, but it clearly didn't trust me and refused to take the water and food I offered.

Mama, though, wouldn't take no for an answer when offering me breakfast.

"Do you think it'll live?" I asked for the hundredth time.

Mama put down her fork and patted my arm. "It's out of your hands. Try to feed it every few hours, but mostly, just let it be."

Wearing overalls and a ragged, sweaty plaid shirt, Daddy came through the back door, looking like he did back on the farm. "Your coop's finished, Tilly," he said with a smile, even acting like the Daddy from long ago back on the farm. He held the kitchen door open for Mama and me to pass through.

The coop was nearly a replica of the one Mama had back in Meadow Springs. The front where the chickens could roam, was a screened pen topped with a tin roof. The back that housed the nesting boxes, was made of wood to keep the chickens warm in winter. A door connected the two.

Mama hugged Daddy tight. She couldn't have been happier if he'd built her a castle. He looked happy too. I wondered if it felt good for him to work with his hands again like back on the farm. Did he miss it? Maybe he was just smiling at the thought of getting back to work in his office. Looking at the chicken coop, even my spirits rose a little remembering that Mr. Lombardi would deliver the chickens today and bring Anne-Marie with him.

"Stack all this in the tool shed." Daddy told me, waving at the lumber, wire and tools scattered around the coop. "I'm going inside to change."

I looked up at my window about to protest, but Mama reminded, "It needs rest."

Storing the wood and wire gave me an idea, but before I could get to work on it, the Lombardis pulled up in their delivery truck. Mr. Lombardi grabbed a bale of straw and helped Mama scatter it in the nesting boxes. I climbed onto the back of the truck bed and pulled the wire cage full of chickens toward me as Anne-Marie pushed it, then came around to help me carry it.

The chickens did not look excited at the prospect of their new home. One pecked me through the slats, drawing blood.

"I'm glad that Leghorn will finally be feasting on someone else," Anne-Marie laughed. "She's a terror."

We dropped the cage in front of the open coop and shooed the chickens inside. Sensing the need to live up to her reputation, the

Leghorn flapped above the Rhode Island Reds and out the coop door. "Grab it!" Anne-Marie yelled as she corralled the other chickens into the coop.

It flapped past Mr. Lombardi delivering another bale of straw at the side gate and headed for the church. Mama joined the chase, but the Leghorn was too fast. I caught it around the middle just as it perched atop the church sign and unloosed an unholy stream of gray poop which trickled over the newly painted letters.

Mama pointed at Daddy's besmirched name and suppressed a laugh. "We better clean that before your father sees it." The Leghorn pecked my hand in protest.

Taking the chicken from me, Mama cradled it at her side, careful to hold one hand under its head so it couldn't peck. "Why, Jessamyn, that's no way to act in your new home."

"So sorry, Signora." Mr. Lombardi helped Mama push Jessamyn into the coop. "The Leghorns. Such tempers they have!"

"She'll soon adjust." Mama said as Mr. Lombardi hoisted the empty cage atop his shoulder. Anne-Marie was given permission to stay, and with Mama adoring her new chickens and Daddy changing out of his old farm clothes, I pulled Anne-Marie upstairs. "Got something to show you."

But Anne-Marie didn't see the bird at first. She only had eyes for the calendar I'd repaired and replaced on the wall, tapping her finger under the June 21 chalked circle. She turned and smiled at me, a smile that illuminated her whole face so bright its rays crossed the distance between us, warmed us both through and pushed yesterday's trouble with Iris into the shadows of days gone by.

I almost forgot about the bird until it gave a wheezy whistle. "What's its name?" Anne-Marie asked.

The bird once again refused my dropper of water. "Don't know." I shrugged. "Haven't given it a name yet. I don't think it likes me. It won't eat. Don't even know if it's going to live."

"Well, he can't be just a no-name bird. He'll never like you if you don't even bother to name him."

"But what if he . . .you know," I said.

"Name him. You won't save yourself any grief at his burial by calling him Bird. Plus, people will think you either have no imagination or never got past the first grade reading primer." I shot her a glance. "I name all the chicks at the feed store as soon as I can tell them apart."

"You name them even though you know they'll get sold?" I asked.

"Well," Anne-Marie rubbed her finger under her nose. "The selling part hasn't been that sure lately, but yeah, I named all those chickens outside." She tapped my window. "The reds are Agnes, Olive, Opal, Gladys, Imogene, and Dorothy."

"Dorothy? That was my best friend back home."

Anne-Marie smiled. "Guess I named her well, then."

"You'll have to tell Mama. She always names her chickens. She'll think she got a bargain, getting the names free in the deal." I pointed at the white one. "And the Leghorn?"

"I heard your Mama call her Jessamyn, but her rightful name is Beelzebub." Laughing, we agreed it was best not to mention that to either parent. "Now, what about your feathered friend?"

I shrugged. "Have you got any ideas?"

"Oh no," Anne-Marie shook her head. "It doesn't work like that. Name's gotta come from your heart."

I raised an eyebrow. "The name Beelzebub came from your heart?"

Anne-Marie held up her bandaged right index finger. "The name Beelzebub came from all the finger peckings."

We both burst out laughing, but try as I might I couldn't think of a good name. Anne-Marie was right. I'd sound like a sap, giving a eulogy for a pet named Bird who hated me.

"Let's try to feed him," she suggested.

Bird hadn't shown the slightest interest in the corn kernels or bits of berry I'd put in the basket, but when Anne-Marie said she had an idea I followed her into the back yard. "Look," she pointed. Gladys was pulling a long, impossibly stretchy worm from the ground inside the chicken coop. "You got something to dig with?"

We found a spade and an old glass pickle jar in the tool shed. It still smelled of dill, but it was unlikely the worm would mind. Since Mama had watered the daisies in the flower bed that morning, I knew the soil there would still be damp.

We sat on the flagstone ledge bordering the flower bed filled with yellow and white daisies that ran under the kitchen and office windows, me with the spade and Anne-Marie with the smelly pickle jar at the ready to hold the worms. I could hear the muffled sound of distant voices through the window above. The shade was pulled to keep out the sun, but the window sash was raised to let the cool morning air in. When I heard the sound of the door opening to Daddy's office, I tapped Anne-Marie and put one finger to my lips. If Daddy was preparing a sermon in his office he'd be annoyed if we disturbed him.

Luckily, it didn't look like we'd be here long. I'd just spotted a long, pink worm and was digging it out when I heard a surprising voice above us. "Reverend Smithfield will certainly be missed," Deacon Westin said. "And not just by the local widows."

Anne-Marie looked annoyed at the sound of Deacon Westin's voice, who I knew she didn't like. Still she had to stifle a giggle when I arranged the pink worm on my palm in the shape of a heart in honor of the past minister's supposed love life.

An unfamiliar voice chuckled. "Yes, he was devoted to the town. Never missed a city hall meeting. Served on the school board back when I was a boy. And involved in every club and fraternity worth its salt."

I pretended to shake salt over the wriggling worm, but Anne-Marie just rolled her eyes.

"Reverend Dewhurst, the area minister, mentioned Pastor Smithfield left very big shoes to fill." Daddy's voice floated out among the daisies. Even though I grinned at Anne-Marie waggling her shoes at me, I felt a twinge of guilt and heard Iris in my head proclaiming at least she wasn't an eavesdropper. But it wasn't planned, so what was the harm?

"That's what we hoped to discuss with you, Reverend," the unknown voice said. "Our last pastor was a member of the Elks." Anne-Marie placed her thumbs against the side of her head and fanned her hands out like antlers. "And he was the Kludd, or chaplain, for our order, The Knights of the Ku Klux Klan. The one putting on the Independence Day picnic your daughter is singing at."

Anne-Marie slowly dropped her hands.

"We'd like to offer the Kludd position to you." Deacon Westin offered. "It's an ideal opportunity to socialize, get to know the leaders in town, and establish your place in Grayson society."

"Almost all the local businessmen are members. All those that count, anyways. Every member has to belong to a local church. A Protestant church, of course," The other voice added. "If they aren't in an appropriate church already, we'll make sure they join your church, Reverend."

Anne-Marie stood up. I grabbed her hand and tried to pull her back down to the ledge. I wished to God that we could go back in time. Wished I'd heeded Iris's voice in my head. Wished me and Anne-Marie had never decided to dig up worms.

"God and country. One hundred percent. That's our motto, Reverend. How about it?"

Daddy's answer was lost in the rush of blood pounding inside my head. Lost in the scuffle as I tried to pull Anne-Marie close while she pushed me away. Lost in the earsplitting snap of a broken friendship as Anne-Marie hissed hoarsely, "I thought you were different," before bolting out our side gate.

CHAPTER 10

ALL MASHED UP

Time doesn't always run in a straight line. Sometimes it veers around you, leaving you stuck in a bubble while everything nearby moves forward without you. The breeze stirs a window shade. A gate swings on its hinge. Voices fade away as people depart. A squawking chicken flaps at a coop door trying to escape. But inside that time capsule a scene replays over and over like a stuck frame of film on a movie projector. A scene you don't want to replay. A scene you can't change. Can't get away from. Can't.

My right hand hurt. I opened my clenched fist and looked at it. A severed worm lay smashed against my palm. Blood oozed from crescent shaped cuts where my nails had punctured the skin.

I trudged up the stairs. Held my palm with its worm offering in front of Bird. "Take it," I pleaded, tears welling in my eyes. Its beak remained clamped. "Take it, you stupid stubborn bird. It's all your fault." I flung the worm into its basket. "Take it!"

I collapsed on my bed and buried my face in the pillow. The scene under the window replayed over and over while time for the rest of the house marched on like usual. The smell of boiled cabbage at supper. The glow of sunset. Darkness. A sound, faintly, faintly creeping through the window from downstairs. chig-ga chig-ga. chig. A dim mechanical drone. chig-ga chig-ga. chig. Needle racing through fabric. Mama treading the sewing machine foot pedals. My choir robe taking shape. Every stitch a stab to my soul. I clamped the pillow tightly around my ears and vowed I'd never wear it.

Mama sewed for an eternity. Sewed me further and further from the possibility of me and Anne-Marie being friends. When it was finally quiet I tossed the hot damp pillow aside and climbed into my tree. I'd missed the sacred sunset. Missed the burnished orange light to illuminate the hymnal pages. But here in my sanctuary I used my voice, my heart, my longing to try to make things right. Squished them all into a prayer pasted together with sobs and sent my S.O.S. soaring up through the leafy canopy. Up there in the infinite indigo yonder I hoped God had a workroom to fix broken things.

A ribbon of light from the hall peered beneath my door followed by a knock.

"Esther?" Mama whispered.

"I'm in the tree."

As I climbed through the window, Mama peered at the bird in the basket. It was too weak to flap or fuss as she examined its wing. "What were you doing in the tree this late?"

"Praying." I said. "Do you think God will heal my bird?"

Mama, with Bird in hand, flipped my light on and held the bird beneath it. "If you're picturing him heaving a blazing miracle bolt down to revive this bird, then I'd say no." I felt my shoulder droop, but Mama winked at me. "I think he already sent the answer to this bird's plea when he sent you to rescue him."

Mama carried the bird in its basket into the kitchen. I followed. "I don't think this wing is broken, just punctured," she said laying the basket on the table. "But if he keeps trying to use it he could do more damage." She handed me a roll of gauze from her apron pocket and a pair of scissors. Gently, she pressed the side with the good wing against her stomach and carefully arranged the hurt one into place. "Cut a strip of gauze about as long as your arm," Mama said. She held the bird in front of her with both hands gently clamping the wing tips in place. "Wrap it around the bird lightly, here right by my fingers. Go around twice. Don't pull." Mama nodded as I followed her directions. "Now take the end and cut it down the center into two strips. Wrap one end under the bandage and back out. Good. Tie it off."

When Mama placed the bird back in its basket, it looked too tired and weak to even fuss. "Get me the cornmeal, a bowl, and the little spoon that goes with the salt cellar," she said while lighting a candle.

Holding the candle, Mama went in the dark back yard, while I assembled what she asked for. She returned with a fat pink worm cupped in her hand. My heart sank as I relived Anne-Marie's accusation.

Mama put the wriggling worm in the bowl. To me she said, "Don't mention this to your father at the kitchen table." To the worm she said simply, "Sorry" before mashing it into a pink-gray paste with the back of the spoon. She stirred in a dab of cornmeal and a drop of water.

"Ready?" Mama asked as she cradled Bird against her. I nodded. "This is for your own good," Mama whispered to the bird as she pinched its beak open. "Quick," she called. I tilted the tiny spoon's pink-gray contents over Bird's beak and watched it slide in. "Again," Mama said and I repeated it.

She placed the wrapped bird in its basket. Without fuss or flap, it settled quietly into the silk scraps. Once again Mama motioned for me to follow. She led me into the parlor and sat at the piano. "When I went into town for fabric today I bought this for you." She handed me a leaflet of sheet music. I read the title, "His Eye is on the Sparrow." Mama smiled. "Seemed appropriate for you."

She played it through once. I sang the refrain the second time through.

"I sing because I'm happy. I sing because I'm free. His eye is on the sparrow. And I know He watches me."

The words flowed over me, as refreshing as raindrops on a dry July day. When we finished, Mama went in the kitchen to wash up. I followed to take my bird upstairs. In the quiet kitchen I watched the still-burning candle beside the basket. Its glow cast a halo around the little bird, a shimmer of light and warmth. Before I blew it out, I drew

Mama beside me, clasped her in a hug, and together we basked in the flicker of hope illuminating one small, helpless bird.

CHAPTER 11

DISAPPOINTED

Things really do look better in the morning. I awoke to the sound of robin song. Wah-wooty-wooty-wooty-woo. I threw back the covers. Glory be! The corn kernels and chopped strawberry were gone. Bird didn't flail or fret when I stood before him. He'd finally got it in his head I was trying to help.

Even better, while I'd been asleep my mind had been tugging at the knot twisted between Anne-Marie and me. The answer was so simple I couldn't believe I hadn't thought of it yesterday. Hope rose inside my heart alongside the sun.

I hurried through my chores. Dodged a peck from Jessamyn while gathering eggs and skipped out the door. As I passed the hopscotch squares where Anne-Marie and I had laughed and jumped backward, the bird's name suddenly popped in my head. A perfect name for a new beginning! Wait until Anne-Marie heard! I marched with such purpose toward the feed store that even when the sweet scent of pink blossoms beckoned from the park, I did not stop to dawdle and daydream. Let some other girl stand on that stage and sing.

If I hadn't been so focused on what I was going to say to Anne-Marie, I'd have noticed it a block away. Big sloppy red words had been inserted in Lombardi's window sign. Lombardi's **Foreign** Feed. **Buy American!** Dribbles of dried red paint dripped down the letters like a bloody nose.

How could someone do such a thing! I ran to the door. A cross had been scratched deeply in its wood. The knob wouldn't turn. Lombardi's Feed was locked. I knocked and knocked but no one answered. "Anne-Marie!" I shouted toward the upper story window "Are you in there?"

No one responded, but I could see a shadow stir near the upstairs curtain. I pounded on the door. "Mr. Lombardi! Anne-Marie! I need to talk to you." I ran back to the front window, pressing my face against the glass beside the hateful scrawling. Inside Mr. Lombardi pushed aside the maroon curtains. When he peeked around the door he held his hand out, barring me from entering.

"What happened? Are you okay?" I demanded.

"A prank," he said. "A foolish prank. No one is harmed." But his eyes, wary and tense, scanned the town square behind me as he spoke.

"I'm so sorry, Mr. Lombardi. I'll help you clean it," I offered.

He waved his hand. "No, child. Thank you, but no."

"Can I see Anne-Marie, please? I need to tell her something."

He shook his head. "That is unwise. I will tell her you asked for her." He withdrew his head to close the door.

I wedged my hand into the door frame. "Wait! Please, who did this?"

The old man smiled forlornly and took my hand in his, pushing it gently back. "Go now. Be safe."

I backed away as he closed the door. He hadn't answered my question, but if I was honest with myself, I already knew the answer.

A strange feeling inched down my spine as I left. A prickle at the nape of my neck crawling down my shoulder blades. Eyes watching up and down the street. Eyes on me. The haberdasher next door arranging his hat sign watched as I walked by. The druggist a few doors down swept the street in front of his pharmacy, eyes tracking me. Mr. Holland, leaned against the Chief, nodding as I passed, but piercing me with his stare. I fought back the urge to run. Placed one foot in front of the other until I reached the safety of our porch.

I woke the next day determined to try Anne-Marie's house again. This time I had a better plan. Grabbing a piece of paper and pencil, I wrote my back up plan. Just in case. Tucking the paper and pencil in my apron pocket, I checked on the newly-named bird. The basket was empty!

Mama and Daddy both came running when they heard my scream. "What is it?" Daddy yelled.

"Lazarus," I cried. "He's missing."

"Who?" Daddy asked. What?"

Mama understood and went straight to my open window, leaning out over the sill and looking down. "Doesn't look like he got out. Would have dropped straight down with his wings bound. He's probably not far." She got down on her knees to look under the bed. Daddy remained in the doorway, his brow still wrinkled in confusion.

I went back to Lazarus's basket on top of the dressing bureau. He had to be nearby. And he was. Snuggled in the fold of my clean nightgown in the top drawer. I'd only left it open a couple of inches last night when I'd dressed for bed, but that was all the space a little robin needed to run away.

"Lazarus?" Daddy said, watching me return him to his basket. "After the man Jesus raised from the dead?" Daddy shook his head and looked at Mama. "That's sacrilegious, don't you agree, Tilly?"

"Instead of fretting over her pet's name, be glad the child knows her Bible." Mama snapped the window sash closed a little harder than she needed to. "Besides, the bird's wing will be well enough for it to fly soon. So you only need stew over it a day or two."

Daddy frowned, but left mollified. Mama's words didn't soothe me at all, though. A day or two?

Before leaving for Lombardi's Feed I took a detour through the back yard to look in the tool shed. Satisfied with what I found, I left by the yard's side gate. Its hinges rasped loudly, causing Jessamyn to squawk in protest.

Lucky for me, Saturday morning the shops were busy. Little children filled the park, shoppers strolled the sidewalks, and store owners waited on customers inside. The hate on Lombardi's window had been scrubbed off. The glass glistened, but the words "Lombardi's Feed" looked dull and worn from the cleansing ordeal. No one noticed me slip down the side alley by Lombardi's Feed and unlatch the delivery gate to the yard where I'd seen Mama and Mr. Lombardi look at chickens. Quietly, I crept around the building and knocked on the back door. No one answered my knock or call. No one peered from between the upstairs curtain.

At least I'd come prepared. Worried I'd get all tongue tied, I'd written down what I wanted to say to Anne-Marie. I took it out to reread it.

Anne-Marie,

I'm sorry. I should have told you about the singing. When I said I'd sing at the Independence Day picnic I didn't know what I know now. Even though you've only known me a couple of days, I hope you'll believe me.

Esther

Before slipping it in the crack between the back door and its frame, I fished the pencil from my pocket and added the number 21 beneath it. Hopefully, Anne-Marie would understand I planned to keep my promise to her, but her family wouldn't.

Leaving the message made me feel better. Maybe it shouldn't have. A note wasn't going to change the hate some people felt towards the Lombardis. And, until Anne-Marie saw the note, things between us wouldn't really be changed. But at least I had done something. I had tried, and I knew I could do more. I refused to celebrate the ugly hate hiding behind the pretty doors up and down the streets in this town. I walked down the town square lighter in the knowledge something in me had changed.

"Hello, Es." I'd have walked right by Westin's Grocery Store without seeing Iris if she hadn't said something. I nodded to her in passing.

"If I were you, I wouldn't be seen at that store." I faced Iris as she continued. "You probably won't find her there again anyway."

"What do you mean? What do you know?"

Iris shifted the twine-wrapped brown paper package in her arms. "I understand they're with family in Muncie. I doubt they'll show their faces until the school board meeting. Father says they'd be wise to just leave."

Leave? That sounded like a threat. Were the Lombardis lives in danger? I turned back toward the feed store with questions spinning in my head.

"Ahem," Iris coughed to get my attention.

I turned back toward her and opened my mouth, but before I could spit out something appropriately spiteful, Iris Westin wrapped her arm around my arm, linking us together like best friends. She waved to her father, visible through their store window as he stood at the cash register and nudged me with her elbow to wave too. She steered me across the street toward the park. When I tried to push her hand off my arm she hissed, "Smile. Like we're friends. Otherwise, I might just spill your secret before the school board meeting. Unless your parents know you're leaving notes for foreigners?" She plopped down on one of the park benches and pulled me beside her.

The words that spilled out of my mouth surprised me even more than her. "You can't blackmail me into being your friend." I talked faster, fearing I'd run out of courage before I ran out of words. "You and me aren't going to be best friends, Iris." She looked startled. "But, we don't have to be enemies, either." I stood up. "I have to go home and . . . and . . . build a cage for my bird."

"Wait!" She pulled my arm. "Let me help."

I was so startled at the thought of Iris Westin wielding a hammer I didn't move while Iris unwrapped her package. The brown paper fell away, revealing a sketchbook and charcoal pencils. Before I could ask what she was doing, she sketched a bird cage. It was a domed cylinder with elaborate scrolled ironwork. She added a swing, mirror and bell.

"There you go, Es" she said. "A plan for your bird cage."

I shook my head. Girl was all arts and no smarts. "I'm not an iron worker."

Iris squirmed and looked at the ground. I started to walk away then turned back. She had tried to help in her own frilly way. "Can I keep the picture anyway?" I asked. "It might not be a plan, but it is a pretty picture." Handing it to me, she smiled, one of her real smiles.

When I got home, Daddy called my name from his office. "I'd like to speak to you." That couldn't be good. He sat behind his desk, sleeves rolled up, glasses slid down the bridge of his nose. "Where have you been?" he asked.

"In town to visit a friend."

"Your mother was looking for you. You forgot to gather the eggs."

"I'm sorry," I said, rising. "I'll apologize to Mama."

"We're not finished," he cut in. "I heard you've been in town several times recently. Make sure you don't neglect your chores, and . . ." he waved me back when I started to rise from the chair again. "Make sure you ask permission before you leave. I don't want you wandering around town, happening upon inappropriate places." He turned to a book lying open beside him.

I knew I'd been dismissed, but I sat there, seething at the unfairness. Inappropriate places! Since when was the feed store an inappropriate place for a girl who grew up on a farm? My father the minister didn't seem to notice some sin going on in town. "Someone painted over Mr. Lombardi's sign. Mean, ugly things," I said. "Did you hear about it?"

"Mr. Lombardi? The man who delivered the chickens?" he asked. "That's terrible. Probably some young hooligans. No doubt liquor had a hand in it too." His eyes strayed back to his book.

"I think it's those men in the masks," I said, willing my voice not to tremble. "Those men who put the 100% American signs in their shop windows. Deacon Westin, maybe."

That sparked his attention. "Do you have any proof of this?" When I remained silent, he said, "I didn't think so. That's how gossip and rumors start. I won't hear any more of this."

"Are you one of them now?" I asked, voice still a-tremble. He looked surprised. "I was in the backyard. I overheard."

"Eavesdropping!" He stood up behind his desk in his ministerial outrage beginning to simmer now. "We have discussed this before. I thought you underst—"

"They're bad, Daddy. How can you let them in the church? You have to know they're bad, like the ones down south you told me about. They put up signs telling you which people to buy from. They want to fire Anne-Marie's mother." I raced on, shocked for the second time today at the words pouring out of my mouth and determined to get in as many as I could. "They don't like people of other religions. Catholics believe in God too, Daddy! They don't like immigrants. The Lombardis could lose their store or wor--"

Daddy slammed his book against the table. "Enough!" He took a deep breath and was quiet for several seconds as he adjusted his eyeglasses and sat down, in an attempt to simmer himself from outrage down to annoyance. "I realize you are worried for your friend, and that is understandable. But I will not tolerate slander." He motioned toward the door. "You are dismissed. I'm disappointed in you, Esther Grace."

Feeling my eyes well with tears, I walked to the door. Before leaving, I turned back ready to speak my mind. But Daddy had clamped his hands on either side of his bowed head, covering his ears.

His eyes were screwed tightly shut, but he looked more like a man in pain than a minister in prayer. As I watched a tear slide down his cheek, I couldn't manage to mumble my disappointment in him too.

CHAPTER 12

CAGED

Does a bird prefer a cage with cool, smooth iron bars better than crude wooden slats? I hoped not, staring at Iris's drawing and then at the old, wooden orange crate I'd pulled from the shed. I laid the leftover coop wire on the grass beside my tools. It was a shame Lazarus wouldn't be able to see the picture pasted on the outside. Such a beautiful, juicy orange half in the farmer's hand, with leafy California citrus trees in the background. I had a feeling he'd like those trees.

It might not be a handsome gilded birdcage like Iris's picture, but this crate was functional and, if I did say so myself, clever. The crate had five wooden sides. All I had to do was cut a piece of wire sheeting to fit over the front, nail one side to the crate and attach a sliver of wood and a loop of wire to the other side for a closure.

I borrowed two custard cups from the kitchen, filling one with chicken feed and the other with water, before taking it upstairs for Lazarus.

My little robin clutched his feet around my finger when I offered it. I was proud he'd come to trust me and hoped he'd like his new home. Carefully, I lifted him into the basket I'd placed inside the cage and fastened the wire door shut. Lazarus strode around the cage floor then stood watching me. I waited for a happy "wah-wooty-wooty-wooty-woo," of thanks, but none came. Still, what remained of my day of rest would be more restful knowing Lazarus couldn't get away.

When I heard Daddy leave to visit Mrs. Tilsbury, down with a bad case of pleurisy, I snuck into his office for a newspaper to line the bottom of the cage. He let me take the old ones to read the

Katzenjammer Kids comics, so I could have asked, but I'd taken care to avoid speaking to him since yesterday.

Two weeks' worth of the *Grayson Herald* were neatly folded and stacked on the book shelf. One for each day we'd lived in Grayson. I removed the bottom one, confident my father had finished it. The front page showed a fiery cross blazing against the night sky. Beside it was a large metal vat that was shaped like a giant vase with a wide bottom. It had a funnel and a long hose. Whole thing had been bashed in the middle. Shattered Mason jars lay scattered around it.

Still Smashed

Buford Diesly, City Desk Editor, *Grayson Herald*

> Acting on a tip from the Women's Christian Temperance Union, police found and confiscated a still on property belonging to Ezra Sawgrass. Thirty-two bottles of bootleg whiskey were destroyed in the raid. Sawgrass's wife, Mable, claimed a mob of white-robed men descended upon the farm before police arrived, beating her husband, destroying property and setting ablaze a large wooden cross. Mrs. Sawgrass could not identify the alleged perpetrators, claiming they wore masks. Sawgrass himself was unable to confirm her story or answer questions at the time of arrest due to injuries he sustained.

Anger welled inside me. I knew Daddy's thoughts on prohibition, but I had never known him to support injuring people. How could he turn a blind eye to what they did? I grabbed his fountain pen and circled the story. Next to it I scrawled "THEY BEAT PEOPLE!" After I arranged it in the middle of his desk, I grabbed another newspaper for Lazarus.

My tree offered little comfort to salve my rile. Its bark chafed like sandpaper. Its canopy confined me within the sun's stifling rays and the wind's parched whistle. The hymnal held no consolation either. Its promises of hope and mercy clouded by images of fiery crosses and dripping red hate. The stifling heat seared my skin, peppered my temper and scorched my Sabbath.

Grateful for Mama's offer of lemonade, I stowed my hymnal and went downstairs. The sunny liquid doused the fire in my throat and revived my spirit.

"Your father wants you to practice your song,"

I took a long gulp of lemonade. "But I don't want to sing."

Mama felt my forehead. "Did you get overheated in that tree?"

I shook my head. " I mean I changed my mind. I don't want to sing at that picnic."

Mama frowned. "You can talk it over with your father tonight. In the meantime, it won't hurt you to sing."

Moving to the piano, Mama spread out the sheet music to "His Eye is on the Sparrow," and motioned for me to sit beside her.

The words "I sing because I'm happy. I sing because I'm free . . ." couldn't have been further from the truth.

I was sitting on my bed encouraging Lazarus to sing when Daddy came in my room. No knock. No "May I come in?" He tossed the circled newspaper on the bed beside me.

"What is the meaning of this?" A vein in his forehead bulged slightly as he frowned at me. I had never seen him so angry.

"I thought you wanted evidence. Proof those masked men do bad things." I stood to return Lazarus to his cage.

"It is not your place to tell me with whom I should affiliate. You are a child. And you have a child's view of the world."

I closed the clasp on the cage and watched Lazarus hop to his water bowl.

"Breaking prohibition is a serious offense, Esther Grace. Alcohol is a danger to our entire society." He tapped the newspaper for emphasis. "This Ezra Sawgrass broke the law."

I turned to face my father. "Does that give men in masks the right to beat him?"

Daddy closed his eyes and sighed. "You don't know—"

"Yes. I do know." I gulped at the lemonade glass beside Lazarus's cage, hoping my mouth and nerves wouldn't dry up. "You know too. They aren't enforcing the law. They're breaking the law. They beat people, threaten people. And now you're one of them!"

Daddy's slap was shockingly strong. Eyes watering, I clasped my red, smarting cheek. The pain was nothing compared to having the trust slapped clean outta my soul. My father had never raised a hand to me. Now a wall stood between us.

His action shocked even him. He stared at his palm still suspended in mid-air, then looked at the floor.

"Please listen," I pleaded.

"No!" He reached his hand out and I flinched. He shook his head, tears glistening in his eyes as he pulled me into an embrace. "No more of this talk. We live here now. It's where God has called me to serve. We don't have to like it, but we have to make the best of it. No more of this disruption, Esther. Look at the hurt it's caused already."

His smooth, starched shirt cooled the sting of my cheek. His hair tonic wafted over me like a balm. Pulling away, he tilted my chin up and brushed a tear from my cheek with his thumb.

"Now I need you to listen," he said pulling away. "Your mother tells me you no longer want to sing at the picnic."

"I can't Daddy. Those people—"

"I said no more of it." He stepped back and inhaled deeply. "You made a promise. People are counting on you." He held up a finger to stifle my interruption. "You will sing. You will practice and you will sing."

He left, shutting the door with a thump. This must be how Lazarus felt when I closed the clasp on his cage.

CHAPTER 13

PROMISES AND PLUCKED CHICKENS

There's a whole book in the Bible with proverbs, or short sayings that teach you something. My father's current favorite is "A man is only as good as his word." He's been working that into a lot of kitchen conversations ever since Sunday. Won't find it in the Bible's Book of Proverbs, though. I looked.

Since promises have apparently been weighing heavily on my father's mind lately, it came as some surprise that he made one involving Mama without her permission. He'd returned from Mrs. Tilsbury's house after arranging with her husband for her funeral today. Her chest pain had gotten worse and her lung collapsed before she died yesterday. While he was there, he'd run into Deacon Westin paying his respects.

"I hope you don't mind, Tilly, but I invited the Westins to dinner Thursday. This Thursday, the 21st," he announced. "The Deacon went on and on about how he was looking forward to one of your home grown chickens."

Mama had just spooned green beans onto his plate. The spoon clattered to the table, scattering vegetables across the tablecloth. By the look on her face, I'd say he was lucky she'd already put the skillet down. "What did you say?" Mama asked.

Daddy repeated himself. "The Westins are having dinner with us tomorrow. I promised them you'd make fried chicken."

In all the eleven years I'd been on this earth, Mama had kept chickens. Never once had one of her girls been plattered and served on our table. Mama did not fry up family.

"Do you mean to say you promised them a chicken dinner without asking me? And one of my chickens?" Mama snatched the fallen spoon from the table and threw it into the frying pan.

"Now dear, it needn't be one of your chickens. Just buy the poultry." He patted Mama's hand. "No one will know the difference."

Mama pulled her hand away. "Buy it from whom, Paul? Westin is the only grocer in town." She jabbed a piece of okra with her fork. "You let him think I'd serve him fresh homegrown chicken. Do you want me to lie to him?"

Before Daddy could answer she added, "And do you think for one minute, Paul Hopkins, that wife of his who fancies herself some kind of prize-winning cook won't question me about every little detail of the meal?" Mama untied her apron and threw it on her seat. "She and her blue ribbons."

Daddy stared at his green beans but didn't touch them. "I've got that funeral to prepare for," he muttered, leaving me with the lunch dishes.

A few minutes after my father left for the funeral, I heard a knock at the back door while I washed dishes. No one ever knocked on our back door. It was Samuel. His battered red wagon stood beside him; an L-shaped pipe fastened to it to form a clothes rod. I recognized Daddy's clean church shirts and Mama's dresses hanging from it.

He tipped his plaid cap. "Your wash." He handed the items to me. "It's fifty-five cents."

"I'll get Mama for you, Samuel" I said, taking the laundry into the kitchen.

"I need the hangers back, please," Samuel called.

Red-faced and puffy-eyed, Mama came to the back door with her pocketbook. She counted out two quarters and a nickel.

"Thank you, Mrs. Hopkins." He tipped his hat. "I'll pick up the dirty laundry again next week."

Mama had nearly shut the door when she stopped abruptly and called out to his retreating back, "Samuel, do you do other jobs? For pay?"

"Well, yes, Ma'am. Depending on the job, that is. What you need doing?'

"Can you butcher a chicken?"

I gasped. Mama ignored me. "I need it done right now. I'll pay . . ." she reached into her pocketbook and pulled out a dollar bill. "One dollar. If you do it right now, that is."

I couldn't contain a second gasp. One dollar was far more than a whole chicken cost at the store, already cleaned and butchered. My frugal Mama wasn't in her right mind.

Samuel smiled broadly. "Yes, Ma'am."

"Wait there one minute," Mama said. She ran from the room and returned fastening her sun hat on. She handed him the dollar and pointed at the coop. "One of the Rhode Island Reds. A fat one. Pluck it, clean it, cut it into pieces." She turned to me. "Get Samuel the axe, a sharp knife, and a bowl for the chicken pieces.

Mama ran toward the side gate. "Wait til I'm gone. Going to church. I can't listen." The gate hinges creaked as she added, "Take the feathers if you think Sophronia can use them for mattress ticking. No sense them going to waste. And any eggs in the hen house."

Suddenly she ran back and grabbed both my hands in hers. "One of the reds. Make sure. Not my Jessamyn."

When the gate slammed behind Mama, I turned to Samuel. "She's kinda excitable today."

I got the axe from the shed. Samuel rolled his sleeves up and pointed at a plump Rhode Island Red pecking at the ground. "How about that one?"

There was no way I was sacrificing Dorothy. "Nuh-uh. Any of the other reds." Samuel caught Beulah as she rested in her nesting box.

Poor thing never was fast. Or smart, for that matter. Jessamyn managed to peck Samuel's hand while Beulah struggled in vain to get away.

As Samuel carried the chicken and axe to the planter ledge I ran inside and closed the door. The thwunk of axe meeting flagstone was followed by the strains of "When we all get to Heaven" floating over from the funeral.

I placed a burlap potato sack and a large bowl outside the back door, careful not to look toward the flying feathers near Daddy's office window. A few minutes later Samuel knocked on the door and handed me the bowl of chicken pieces. He loaded his bag of feathers into the wagon and nestled two eggs atop it. Feathers clung to his hair and shirt. Blood was smudged along his jaw, but he wore a wide grin as he said goodbye, with his dollar and fifty-five cents stowed in his pocket.

Even though it pained me, I took a bowl of water and a rag outside to the planter ledge. I planned to save Mama the pain of seeing Beulah's sacrificial altar. But Samuel had already beaten me to it.

From the other side of the gate I heard a loud voice. I put the water down and opened the gate. Deacon Westin held Samuel by a fistful of overall straps.

"Now I'm going to ask you one more time, boy. What you been up to in that back yard?" He spoke the words inches from Samuel's face.

"I was doing work for Mrs. Hopkins." Fear shone on his face.

"You're lying, boy. Both Miz Hopkins and the Reverend are in the church right now. Just came from there myself. Funeral."

"Please, sir, if you'll just go ask her." Samuel cast his eyes downward. "Mrs. Hopkins will tell you. I butchered a chicken for her."

The Deacon looked toward the trickle of mourners exiting the church and laughed. "Butcherin' chickens, huh? I think you saw nobody was home. Thought you'd help yourself to a nice plump chicken, huh?" He pointed to the wagon. "I see those eggs in your wagon, boy. Bet I'll find the chicken in that bag, its neck wrung for your dinner." He licked his lips. "Do you know what we do with thieving, no-good types like you 'round here?"

"Miss Esther," Samuel raised his eyes to meet mine. "Tell him, Esther." His voice shook as he added, "Please."

Deacon Westin turned to me, Samuel still in his grip. I opened my mouth, dry as cotton. Not a single word came out. I sputtered. Coughed. Finally, I nodded.

Samuel's eyes didn't stray from the ground. "I was hired, sir. Esther knows." I managed another shaky nod as he finished addressing the dirt. "I don't want no misunderstanding, sir."

Mr. Westin slowly released his grip on Samuel. Looking from his prey to me, the deacon withdrew a peppermint from his pocket and popped it in his mouth. I could hear Samuel's breath coming in short fast spurts.

"You see there ain't no misunderstanding in the future, boy." He thumped Samuel on the chest. Even from three feet away I could smell his breath, hot and minty as he hissed in Samuel's face, "You hear me?"

Samuel drew a ragged breath. "Yes. Yes, sir." He nodded then slowly backed away, one wagon wheel creaking loudly behind him as he walked, eyes fixed on the ground.

Still I stood, trapped in shame and humiliation. Hating my tied tongue. Loathing my weak spine. Hearing in my ear, "A man's only as good as his word." What good was a girl who couldn't wrangle up her words when it counted?

Deacon Westin took off his straw hat, fanned himself and smiled broadly at me. "Sure is hot today, isn't it, Esther?"

CHAPTER 14

GOOD GIRL

There's nothing in this world more useless than unsaid words. You can try to bolster your pride afterward by thinking of what you should have said. I was good at that. You can save and store those unused words for the future, stacking them like firewood for winter. I've tried that, but when the time comes to use those words, my tongue won't spark the tinder to light the fire. Mostly, you just blame yourself for being a big ole dry-mouthed coward. At that one, I excelled.

Yesterday's shameful silence still buzzed my head like a horsefly circling fresh manure. All the words I should have said whirred through my brain. *"Leave Samuel alone!" "You've no business talking to him that way!" "How dare you, Deacon Westin!"* All brave words. All unsaid words. All useless. Truth be told, I was too scared to let those words loose on Deacon Westin.

More shame awaited me at the piano, when, by Daddy's orders, I had to practice my song. Had to accompany myself on the piano since Mama was busy preparing for tonight's dinner. Had to sing like I meant it about being happy and free. Worst of all was what was coming tonight. Not dinner with the Westins, even though that was sure to be dreadful. It was admitting to Anne-Marie that she was right. I wasn't different. Just cowardly. I'd be in a white robe singing come Independence Day and there wasn't anything I could do about it. At least I could keep my promise and be there with her tonight at the meeting. Maybe that counted for something?

The doorbell rang as I practiced my song in the parlor. I was surprised to see Mr. Lombardi, hat in hand, on our porch step.

"Good morning. Please, may I speak to Signora Hopkins?"

"Mama's busy in the kitchen. I'll call her in a minute." I stepped onto the porch and closed the door behind me. "First, will you please tell me how Anne-Marie is?"

The elderly man stroked his mustache as he sized me up with his eyes. "Please, Mr. Lombardi. I'm worried about Anne-Marie."

He said, "Anne-Marie has been sad. Upset. First the worry for her madre. Then the window." He traced one finger down the brim of his hat and the crinkles around his eyes softened. "But today, when we return from Muncie, she is brighter. A friend's note will do that." He smiled at me.

"Can I see her?" I asked.

He shook his head. "No. It is not safe to have visitors now." Before I could object, he raised his index finger. "We see after the school board meeting. Perhaps."

I crossed my arms, ready to disagree, but Mr. Lombardi continued. "I will tell Anne-Marie her stubborn friend with the big heart misses her and wishes her well. You tell your madre ten more chickens are coming around the 28th. I will deliver them the next morning." He stood and placed his hat on his head.

I crossed my arms. "I'll give Mama the message after I see Anne-Marie."

Mr. Lombardi smiled "You remind me of my nipotina. Two peas in a pod." He winked at me before descending the porch stairs. "I think you will give your madre the message because you are a good girl." He lifted his hat in salute and left.

Mama was surrounded by baking pans, apples, and sugar when I gave her the message. She walked to the window, hands dusted with flour and looked out the glass at her chickens. "Ten more? Sixteen will make a nice family." She bit her lip. "But it won't make up for Beulah." A single tear rolled down her face and she brushed it away with a floury finger, leaving a white streak down her cheek.

I hugged her. "Let me help," I offered. Mama nodded toward the bowl of peas on the kitchen table. "You can shell the peas."

As I slit the pods with my finger and pushed the peas in the big blue bowl, I thought about Mr. Lombardi's words. "Two peas in a pod." I liked the idea of Anne-Marie and me being two of a kind, side by side. But peas get split apart, tossed around, and gobbled down. Lord, let the two of us stay side-by-side friends! I couldn't bear to lose another friend so soon after losing Dorothy.

Mama handed me the pie dough, wrapped in waxed paper, to chill in the ice box. As I put it on the top shelf, I spied what was left of Beulah. She lay in a baking pan coffin covered with a tea towel, but one corner was turned back, revealing her goose-pimpled, naked flesh soaking in buttermilk. I looked at Mama pulling the apple peeler from the cabinet and wondered why she hadn't just bought a chicken. She'd been bullied into something she didn't want to do. Just like me.

I helped Mama clamp the peeler on the edge of the table. We took turns cranking the handle, watching each apple turn on its core as a thin ribbon of green peel was shaved away. Mama won the contest to see who could peel the longest apple peel ribbon without breaking it. The prize was the pie crust cookie: a crisp flaky cookie fashioned out of leftover pie dough trimmings, brushed with butter and sprinkled with sugar and cinnamon. She'd peeled nearly six feet! I only managed two, but I was confident Mama'd share half that cookie when it came out of the oven.

Mama consulted the McCalls magazine cover as she cut a perfect apple and leaf shape from dough to decorate the top of the pie. "Careful," Mama warned as I crimped the edges like the recipe picture showed. "I want those edges nice and even like the picture."

I'd never known Mama to be vain or prideful, but watching her carry that pie to the oven like it was a fragile treasure, I wondered if Mama wanted to best Mrs. Westin at her own game just this once. As we tidied up and snacked on apple peels, I slipped my arms around Mama's skinny middle and kissed her flour streaked cheek, determined to not leave my praise unsaid and useless. "You sure made a beautiful pie, Mama."

We baked biscuits, cooled the pie and buttered the peas, but when it came time to fry the chicken, Mama shooed me out of the kitchen despite my protest. With the table set, and everything else ready, Mama insisted there was no more work for me to do. I knew better. I even offered to cook the chicken myself, but Mama turned me down. In a strange way, I think she felt like it wouldn't be dignified for anyone else to handle Beulah. Nobody else was going to batter and fry one of her girls. And nobody was going to watch Mama do it, either.

The Westins arrived as Mama took the last drumstick out of the frying pan. It smelled heavenly. The table looked beautiful with the Blue Willow china on our best white tablecloth and platters of chicken, biscuits and peas. A sparkling cut crystal vase, a wedding present from Grandma Lloyd, held daisies from the backyard. The pie, in all its glory, sat in the middle of the table, doing Mama proud, looking just like the McCalls magazine picture!

After Daddy said grace, the platters began circulating hand to hand. Mama passed the chicken platter to me without taking a piece. I considered taking Beulah's wing, but its tip, fried golden crisp, pointed accusingly at me. I sighed and passed the chicken to Iris.

As we ate, Mrs. Westin talked about the upcoming county fair. Lemon cream pound cake! She said it with a great big exclamation mark as though we should all clasp our hands to our hearts and swoon. The juice of six lemons, a tablespoon of freshly grated lemon peel, a cup of sour cream and –gasp—a little secret she simply couldn't reveal until the ribbon presentation.

"That sounds delightful, Margaret, dear." Mr. Westin patted her hand. "Reverend, there's a few of the boys I'd like you to meet tonight. Some of the local businessmen who go to the Methodist church."

I dropped my fork. Peas escaped and rolled toward Iris. "You're going to that meeting, Daddy?"

His look signaled I better proceed with caution. "Yes. I am attending the school board meeting."

"But you're not on the school board. Why do you need to go?" My father wiped his face with his napkin, returned it to his lap, and stared at me for several seconds before not answering.

"Deacon," he said. "Have you seen Mr. Tilsbury since the funeral? I should stop by and visit him tomorrow."

The deacon's mouth was too full of fresh homegrown chicken to answer, so he shook his head.

When the dinner plates were cleared I filled everyone's coffee cups. Mama hovered a knife over her beautifully decorated pie, asking, "Who'd like a slice of freshly-baked apple pie?"

I wasn't about to let Mama's moment of baking glory go unnoticed. "It's beautiful, Mama," I said. "And delicious too!" I looked around the table and assured everyone, "Mama's pies are always delicious."

"I'll take some of that pie off your hands, Mrs. Hopkins," Deacon Westin offered. "Looks mighty tasty!"

Daddy gratefully accepted the next piece. "Well done, Tilly. It looks very elegant. Perhaps you should enter it in the county fair!" Daddy suggested. I smiled even though Daddy was not currently in my good graces.

"Oh, I don't think they allow entries copied from magazines," Mrs. Westin said. "Only original culinary creations. But I've been meaning to try that McCall's recipe myself, so I'll sample yours." She handed her dessert plate to Mama.

The smile fell from Mama's face and her hand trembled as she accepted Mrs. Westin's plate and placed a wedge of pie on it. I wasn't sure in that moment who I hated more: Mr. or Mrs. Westin.

"How is your solo coming along?" Mr. Westin asked between shoveling in bites of pie. "Your debut is less than two weeks away now!"

Looking down at my uneaten pie, I tried to gather my courage.

After a long silence Daddy said, "Mr. Westin asked you a question."

I took a bite of pie. Even though I knew it to be juicy and delicious, it was dry as sawdust in my mouth. I took a gulp of water and coughed.

"She's been practicing," Daddy said. "What's the title, Tilly?"

Mama looked up from her pie. "His Eye is on the Sparrow."

"That's it," Daddy said. "She sounds wonderful."

I gulped more water. *A man's only as good as his word.* Licked my lips. *A man's only as good as his word.* I squeezed my eyes closed and blurted "I've changed my mind. I can't sing after all."

Daddy nearly spit his pie out.

"What?" Apple juice dribbled from the corner of Deacon Westin's mouth. He turned to my father. "She can't back out now! Plans have been made. Circulars printed, for god's sake!" He pointed his fork at me, a crumb of golden crust still clinging to one tine. "Why, any girl in this town—no--any girl in this county would be honored to be in your place, girl!" For a moment I feared he'd throw the fork at me like a spear.

Daddy stood up. "Now wait, Deacon. Esther and I have already discussed this. She's just got a little stage fright, that's all." I stared at my father, surprised that in his shame of me, he'd lie and break the ninth commandment. "She'll sing as promised."

Mr. Westin tapped his dirty fork on our white tablecloth. "You see she . . ."

"Pardon me," Iris interrupted. "May I be excused?" She lifted her hand to her temple. "I'm suddenly not feeling well."

"Take her to your room, Esther," Mama offered. "She can lie down until it's time to go home."

Iris leaned against my arm and shuffled slowly out of the kitchen with my assistance, assuring her mother she'd be fine after a short rest. Until we reached my room upstairs. Where she promptly dropped the weak, fainting act, walked over to Lazarus's cage and tapped it. "Did you build this?"

"What was that all about?" I asked. "You don't look sick."

"I was struck with a terrible headache," Iris said, plopping herself on my bed in a flounce of yellow silk and ribbons. "It came on suddenly while listening to my friend say stupid things that will get her in trouble."

Sitting down beside her on the bed, I felt a tiny surge of respect for Iris. "Thank you," I said, meaning it. She smiled, and I could tell she meant it, too.

"Tell me you're not going to that meeting tonight, Es."

I sighed. "Listen, if we're going to be not-enemies, or friends, or whatever, you gotta get my name right. Two syllables. Es-ter."

"Tell me you're not going to that meeting tonight, Esther."

At that moment, Mrs. Westin called for Iris from downstairs. It was time for them to leave. Almost time for me to leave, too, if I was going to make it to the school board meeting by 6:00.

"Listen," Iris whispered. "Stay away from that meeting. Stay away from that girl. And stay away from that feed store. Things could happen. Bad things, Es. I'm telling you. As your friend."

CHAPTER 15

CURTAINS

I've always prided myself on my ability to sneak around unnoticed. If you're thinking minister's daughters don't do those kinds of things, well, you'd be wrong. With less than two weeks as the minister's daughter under my belt, I've found it the perfect cover. People think we're innocent, busy embroidering decorative pillows and memorizing scripture instead of scrambling down trees and going to meetings we're not supposed to be at.

After Reverend Daddy left with the Westins, I told Mama I was tired and needed to lie down. A glance at the grandfather clock in the parlor told me it was 5:52. Eight minutes! I arranged my boots at the foot of my mattress, stuffed sweaters inside my winter coat to form a torso and pulled the covers over it to make the outline of a body. I pushed off the light and held a finger up to shush Lazarus when he chirped, then climbed quietly out of the tree.

Halfway down I realized the fault in my plan. Mama's profile was clearly visible through the window as she stood at the sink washing dishes. The minutes ticked away as I considered what to do. I chewed my lip, said a prayer and decided to chance it. Quickly and quietly I dropped out of the tree.

Quick as a firefly's wink, I scooted to the side of the house and flattened myself against the building. Hugging the wall, I crept along until I was directly next to the door. It was wide open. I peeked around it and saw Mama turn to reach for a dish towel. I dashed across the open space, nimble as a cat. A few more steps and then the window. I dropped to my knees and crawled below the window, out of Mama's sight. Above me, I heard the slosh of water and chink of drinking glass jostling drinking glass floating from the open window.

I crept a few more feet hugging the wall. Safe! I ran for the gate, cursing inwardly as it groaned on its hinges. Hopefully, Mama had enough on her mind between poor Beulah and the McCall's pie fiasco that she wouldn't notice the noise.

The best way to not attract attention to yourself is to just walk calmly, but I was in a big hurry with only a couple of minutes left. Main Street was quiet. Most of the shops were closed and people had settled into their homes for dinner. So, I ran for it. Pounded the pavement until I saw the school a block away. I slowed down. Caught my breath. The auditorium was obvious. A big building with a crowd gathered around the open doors. Men mostly. The meeting must not have started yet, since several of them held glowing lit cigarettes and talked in small groups. Time to be careful. Instead of walking toward the auditorium I veered toward the play yard on the left. People probably wouldn't be suspicious of a kid at the play yard. I waited behind a big tree, watching the doors to the auditorium.

Daddy and Mr. Westin must have already gone inside. I didn't see the Lombardis either. When the last man ground out his cigarette and entered the auditorium, I ran toward the back of the building.

Anne-Marie was nowhere in sight. I whispered her name and peeked around the corner of the building, but the only thing behind the auditorium were three steps leading down to a back door. It was ajar. As I opened the door, the evening sun shed a swath of weak light along the jumble of scenery, racks of clothing, and cast-off furniture. It resembled a rag picker's junk shop. When I shut the door behind me, I was plunged into darkness.

In the distance I heard the murmur of voices. "Anne-Marie?" I whispered. "Are you here?"

A sliver of bright light opened ahead and the voices grew louder. Someone whispered," Shh!"

Arms fanned ahead of me to avoid running in to something, I made my way toward the long sliver of light. After bumping against something tall and furry, I panicked, then calmed down after realizing the thing with fur wasn't breathing. I decided to wait a moment and allow my eyes to adjust to the dimness. In a minute I was able to discern it was a tall paper mache rabbit, standing on its hind legs. It was covered in bristly fabric, wearing a silver tin crown and holding a scepter. I made out Anne-Marie's silhouette next to the sliver of light and moved toward her.

The voices were clearer now. Anne-Marie held one finger to her lips and pointed for me to stand on the other side of the light. I could now see it was coming from the thin crack between the heavy velvet stage curtains. Anne-Marie pinched the thin curtain gap together and cupped her hand around my ear, whispering, "Don't say a word. The school board is on the other side of the curtain. Be careful."

I nodded, wishing I could see something besides the curtains. Anne-Marie had one eye glued to the tiny gap between them, blocking my view. But I didn't call myself a sneak for nothing; I tapped her and pointed below her, then laid on my stomach between her legs and peeked through the gap at the very bottom of the curtain. Anne-Marie smiled down at me.

Only the backs of those seated on the stage were visible since they faced the audience. The woman speaking had a soft voice, which made it hard to understand, but I soon gathered she was talking about new math books. They must not have gotten to the business with Mrs. Lombardi yet. I scanned the faces of the people in the auditorium. Fifty or so occupied seats in the sloped auditorium. Most were in clumps of three or four, seated near the stage. Spying my father and Mr. Westin in the second row, I caught my breath. A man I didn't know sat with them. I watched my father's impassive face as the woman droned on about more challenging division problems.

Mrs. Lombardi, along with her in-laws, sat in the front row on the opposite side. Several women sat nearby. The other side of the aisle, where my father sat, was composed entirely of men. Perhaps the other women were Mrs. Lombardi's fellow teachers, here to support her. I certainly hoped so, feeling ashamed my father wasn't beside her, lending his backing.

There followed an equally boring, but thankfully brief, discussion on installing new chalkboards. The secret inner workings of the school office and teachers' lunch time had always intrigued me. Turns out it was even more boring than schoolwork.

The last item on the agenda was finally called: the disciplinary hearing of Mrs. Civilla May Lombardi, sixth grade teacher. The atmosphere in the auditorium changed instantly. People sat up straighter and leaned forward. A man in a brown suit stood from his place at the center of the table and began to read from a document.

"I hold in my hand a petition signed by twenty-two parents of Grayson Primary School pupils. It reads as follows:"

> "We demand the immediate termination of Mrs. Civilla Lombardi on the grounds she is indoctrinating our children in the Catholic faith. In keeping with the tenets of her faith, Mrs. Lombardi encourages obedience to the pope, making her teachings incompatible with democracy and the inculcating of loyal American citizens."

"Now, the board would like to—"

"Excuse me." Mrs. Lombardi stood, straightened the cuffs of her sleeves and addressed them in a voice loud and clear as a bell. "You have not completed the reading of the document. If you would please read the signatures."

"That is not necessary, Mrs. Lombardi." The man shook the paper at her. "The fact that there are twenty-two signatures speaks for itself."

Mrs. Lombardi rose again. "The Sixth Amendment gives me the right to be confronted with the witnesses against me." Her stern brown eyes swept the audience.

The entire room waited on the edge of their seats. The man conferred with those on either side of him. After some seconds Mrs.

Lombardi began reciting the constitutional amendment aloud by memory, ending with "Of course, it refers to a jury trial, but as an institution that prides itself on inculcating democracy, I'm sure the school board will uphold the rights outlined in the Bill of Rights in this hearing."

Finally, after more conferring, the man read aloud the twenty-two names. Mr. Holland, both of the Westins and six more names from church were familiar. Thank heavens Daddy's name was not among them!

The man continued, "These are serious charges." He paused to allow members of the audience to nod and shout agreement. "The board would like to—"

Mrs. Lombardi stood once more. "Serious charges, indeed," she agreed. "For the record, please explain the cause."

Throwing his document on the table, the man said, "Cause? What are you referring to?"

Mrs. Lombardi smiled. "I'm referring to the Sixth Amendment which I just recited. I'm inquiring to the cause of these charges. I assume there must be some witnesses or sworn statements documenting these serious charges." She paused as the man's head swiveled again toward his colleagues, then continued. "If so, they should come forward so that my counsel and I may question them and their statements be investigated, as guaranteed in the Bill of Rights."

"Counsel?" One of the members at the table exclaimed.

"Now see here, Civilla, this little act has gone far enough." The man strode across the stage to face her.

"Act?" A well-dressed woman in an ostrich feathered cloche hat sitting beside Mrs. Lombardi rose, holding a pad of paper and pencil. "Do I understand the principal of this school considers the enforcement of constitutional rights an act?"

"Listen to her!" the man beside my father shouted. Pointing at the women on the opposite side he yelled, "Three years they've had the right to vote and now they think they can shoot their mouths off about the constitution." I recognized that voice! The man with Deacon Westin in my father's office.

Another man with a bushy mustache stood and yelled, "Americans stand for America. You Roman Catholics only care about Rome." Several voices erupted in support. "Papists!" "She'll only listen to the Pope!" "She's no Christian." "Dirty immigrants—just like those Irish." As the women stood to address these insults, the mustached man added, "Why don't you go back to where you came from?"

Chaos erupted throughout the auditorium. Yelling, finger pointing, jeering across the aisle that separated the two sides.

Anne-Marie snapped the curtains together and whispered, "She's got them going now. They're playing right into her hands."

Several loud bangs erupted from the stage. Anne-Marie and I inched the curtain open enough to see again. A stooped elderly man on the end of the table pounded a gavel on the table repeatedly.

"Order!" he shouted. "There will be order!" He motioned for the brown-suited principal to sit. "As a former history teacher, I would like to thank Mrs. Lombardi for her enlightening lesson on the Bill of Rights. As the superintendent of instruction for this county, I shall add to her tutorial by reminding those assembled here today of the First Amendment, which guarantees the freedom to practice the religion of one's choice."

Mr. Westin booed loudly. The elderly man pointed the gavel at him. "You will be silent or you will be expelled from these proceedings." I smiled watching Mr. Westin squirm in his seat. "Our constitution lesson completed, if anyone has direct knowledge and documented proof of Mrs. Civilla Lombardi's proselytizing children, trying to convert them to Catholicism, during school hours, stand now and be heard for the record."

The male half of the auditorium eyed one another and shifted in their seats. The speaker continued, "And, may I remind you, hearsay and gossip do not qualify as proof." After a moment's further silence he banged his gavel and turned to those seated on the stage with him. "No witnesses have come forward. All those in favor of dismissing these charges raise your hand." Seven of the nine members raised their hands. "Those in favor of terminating Mrs. Lombardi's employment raise your hand." Only the principal responded. The elderly man pointed his gavel at the one man who had not voted and frowned. "For the record, one abstention. Charges are dismissed and this meeting is adjourned." He banged his gavel once more for good measure.

Anne-Marie pulled me to my feet and wrapped me in a hug. "She did it! Mama's going to be alright!"

"I'm so glad!" I whispered. But Anne-Marie pushed me away playfully and joked, "You shouldn't be. Now you'll have to put up with her for the whole school year! She's tough. You're in for a lot of homework in sixth grade."

At that moment there was a swooshing sound to the left of us and the stage curtains began to glide open.

CHAPTER 16

PRETENDING

Lord, help us sinners and sneaks! I grabbed Anne-Marie and pushed her to the left. We dove into a rack filled with costumes, trying to hide our limbs and faces behind butterfly wings and gnome hats. A large shaft of light now spilled backstage from the auditorium.

All the board members who had voted to dismiss charges walked past, chatting about the meeting. Frozen in place, we watched them exit out the back door I'd come through.

When they'd exited, Anne-Marie whispered, "Bet they don't want to face some of the audience." She pointed to eight men standing in the aisle speaking to the principal. Daddy stood beside them, near Deacon Westin. He shook hands with them and left by the auditorium door. The remaining men resumed their huddle. The Lombardis and their female friends were no longer in the room.

"There goes my father," I whispered. "I gotta get home."

"Me too. I'll be in big trouble if Mother gets home and finds me gone." Anne-Marie hugged me again. "Thank you for coming!"

"I promised I would. That's what friends do, you know."

Anne-Marie smiled. "Well, thank you for being my friend."

My heart felt as warm as the center of chocolate cookie fresh out of the oven. I hoped she'd still feel that way when she found out I was still scheduled to sing at Independence Day. I'd have to own up to it, but this didn't seem like the right time. "If we keep to the edges where it's darker and the curtains are bunched up, I think we can get out of here without being seen." I pulled her along the edge of the wall, skirting a shadowy forest of flat wooden tree props and clay pots of rainbow-colored tissue paper flowers.

"Fairy Kingdom play last spring," Anne-Marie whispered with a giggle. We were almost to the back door when Anne-Marie bumped into the huge rabbit standing upright on his hind legs. Clang! Its tin crown clattered to the floor, and its scepter rolled across the stage toward the audience.

"What's going on back there?" I recognized the principal's voice. He strode toward the stage. "Who's back there?"

I threw a gnome hat at Anne-Marie and clamped one over my head to cover most of my face. "Run!" I hissed.

Throwing the back door open with a bang, we tossed the hats behind us, abandoned all caution, and sprinted across the play yard toward the far side of the school. As we rounded the corner I nearly knocked over the elderly superintendent of instruction man. He reached for my arm to steady himself. We reached out to help him, but he waved our hands away, clearly annoyed. "What are you doing here? It's nearly dark. Too late for pupils to be on the play yard!"

Relief flooded through me. He thought we were just out playing late.

"We're sorry, sir," Anne-Marie said. "We're on our way home now." Not even a lie! She was good!

I grabbed Anne-Marie's hand to make a run for it. "See that you walk!" The old man gave us a stern look then shooed us toward the street.

"That was close!" I smiled at Anne-Marie then froze. Fifty yards away, a man in a gray suit stood leaning against the door of the school office. He was staring at us. My breath caught in my throat, and I spun Anne-Marie around so neither of us were facing him. "It's the man who was yelling about women voting." I whispered. "He's watching us." I started to walk quickly, pulling Anne-Marie along. "If we get caught, we were just playing on the playground, agreed?" When Anne-Marie nodded, I added, "We've even got the superintendent of instruction as our witness."

Anne-Marie tugged me to the right. "There's a shortcut by the Harper's house." We ran. When it was time to split up, I said, "Let's meet at the park benches at noon tomorrow."

By the time I reached home, the sun was sinking low on the horizon. Seeing the parlor was dark, I breathed a sigh of relief. Maybe my father had stopped on the way home. The hinges creaked as I opened the gate. If I was going to lead a life of sneakery and deception, I should oil that blasted gate.

The kitchen light was ablaze, but I couldn't tell if Mama was in there. I dashed to the wall and crept under the planter box below Daddy's darkened office. That was a promising sign. He'd probably stopped at Mr. Tilsbury's house. My hopes were dashed when I crept toward the kitchen window. Voices. Two of them. Mama and Daddy must be sitting at the table. I inched along the wall until I was two feet from the window then dropped to my belly and crawled on my knees and elbows under the window. Silently, I inched along, then stopped.

" . . . understand you want her to keep her word, but what's the harm in letting her back out of singing? You did tell her when she accepted that it was her choice."

"She made her choice, Tilly. A person's only as good as his or her word." My father had a thing about keeping his word, especially to God, which is exactly what landed us here in Grayson with a bunch of people who twist God's word to practice hate.

And here I was, eavesdropping yet again. I looked up. *I swear I don't plan it, Lord!* It just comes with the territory when you're under windows or hidden in trees.

I pictured the two of them sitting at the table, coffee cups in hand. I debated: keep moving or wait to see if they say more? I decided to wait. Not to eavesdrop, but because it would be darker. More coverage to run to the tree. One of the chickens began clucking. Jessamyn met my gaze. Our eyes locked. *Just this once*, I prayed, *stay quiet!* I held my finger to my lips and smiled at Mama's pet chicken.

She cocked her head to the side, quieted down and stared back at me. *Nice chicken!*

"Maybe I was harsh. I'll go up and check on her. She'll be anxious to hear the good news about her friend's mother." Daddy's chair scraped against the linoleum as he stood.

I scrambled on knees and elbows to get past the window. I'd never make it in time. I sprinted toward the tree.

"Buck-buck-buck-buck-buck!" Jessamyn gave it her all, flapping, screeching and launching herself at the coop door to tattle on me.

I hoisted myself onto a branch just as my father opened the back screen door. Flattening myself against the trunk, I held my breath.

He walked to the coop. "That bird's a menace. Why couldn't you have done us all a favor and cooked that one?"

The sound of a fry pan slamming down on the kitchen counter startled me. "Why don't you do us all favor, Paul Hopkins, and stop worrying so much about what others think about the new minister and his family. You should have never invited them over for dinner. We're never going to fit in their imaginary perfect minister's family mold."

"Now, Tilly, honey, you know I—"

Mama cut him off. "That goes for you too, Paul. You're trying so hard to fit in here. To live up to the deacons' expectations. I'm not sure I like Reverend Hopkins nearly as much as I liked Farmer Hopkins. The sad thing is, I think you feel the same way. You don't trust your own instincts here, Paul. You follow when you ought to lead."

I sucked in my breath, imagining Daddy's face when Mama delivered those words. Silence floated out the kitchen window, then a loud sniff followed by quiet murmurs that I couldn't make out. After a minute I heard Mama whisper quiet as the rustle of a warm blanket, "Trust yourself, dear. You can do this."

I felt guilty listening in on this private conversation between my parents, but I couldn't pull myself away. It was quiet again for a moment, then I heard the sound of chair legs scraping against the linoleum and more soft murmuring.

Yikes! What if they come upstairs to check on me? I shimmied up the tree and through the window. Threw back the covers, tossed armfuls of boots and sweaters into the wardrobe and flung myself in bed. No time to remove my shoes or change into my nightgown. Heart racing, I tucked the blanket tight around me and closed my eyes pretending to sleep.

I'd made it! Darkness enveloped my bedroom. A cool evening breeze whispered through the curtains. Lazarus chirped quietly in his cage. I yawned and adjusted my pillow, waiting for Daddy to come upstairs. After a while, exhaustion crept over me, and I no longer had to pretend I was sleeping.

CHAPTER 17

NOTED

Great days start with pancakes. Hot, springy, spongy buttermilk manna straight from heaven via Mama's frying pan. Melting butter oozing across the top, maple syrup dripping down the sides. Mmm-mmm, they were good! My spirits soared. Last night's outing a success. Anne-Marie and I back on good terms. There was still the pesky business concerning telling her the singing was back on, but in less than two weeks I'd have the singing behind me and nothing to worry about.

I sliced a wedge of pancakes, dripping with goodness, and popped them in my mouth. Daddy put down his newspaper. "I have good news about your friend's mother." I wondered if he even remembered her name.

"The school board has decided to keep Mrs. Lombardi." Smiling, he leaned toward me. "You see, if you just trust in the system it will all work out for the best!"

I nodded and smiled back even though I was still annoyed at him for not standing up to the hateful bullies in town. Pancakes tend to make me more charitable than usual.

"Now about that singing commitment, if you see it through I think you'll find—" He was interrupted by a loud knock at the front door. Mama answered the door and called for Daddy. Probably Mr. Tilsbury, though he was awful early, even for a mourner, in my opinion. Surely grief could wait until after pancakes.

As I rinsed off my breakfast plate, Daddy returned. The smile was gone from his face. "Sit down, Esther Grace. I want to talk to you." My middle name was not a good omen. "You should hear this, too," he told Mama. "That was Dr. Arnell at the door." I searched my memory but came up blank on the name. "He saw two girls running away from the school after the meeting last night. He recognized Mrs. Lombardi's daughter. Bud wasn't sure, but he thinks the other girl might have been you. He said the girl resembled the photograph in my office."

The tap continued to pour water in the sink behind me. Mama reached over me to turn it off.

"I want the truth." Daddy said. "You told your mother you were going to lie down. Were you with the Lombardi girl last night?"

"She was in bed, Paul. You saw her yourself, remember?" Mama asked.

The morning sun glinted on Daddy's gold wire-rimmed glasses like a spark. I had the lie all ready. Had stacked the words like a pile of firewood. The playground. The superintendent of instruction. But as I thought it over I realized they were flimsy lies. They'd fall like a house of cards.

I took a deep breath. "Yes. It was me. I made her a promise I'd be there. I had to keep my promise . . . you're always telling me to keep my word."

"I see." Daddy pushed his glasses up the bridge of his long, thin nose and stared out the back door. "You're forbidden to see her again outside of school." I started to protest as he continued. "The girl is clearly a bad influence. As punishment, you'll not leave the house until the Independence Day celebration. You'll practice your song and help your mother with chores."

"It's not fair," I said, tears welling in my eyes. "She's my friend. I promised her. What about a man's only as good as his word?"

He shook his head, refusing to rise to the bait of his own words. "One more thing. You climbed down the tree last night, didn't you?"

No lie would help me now. I nodded.

"If you use that tree again for some nefarious outing, I will take an axe to it and cut it down. Mama gasped right along with me. "I will not have my daughter seen lurking about in the shadows engaging in activities unbecoming the minister' family."

My tree! Anything but my tree!

"That's a little extreme, don't you—" Daddy stormed out of the kitchen before Mama could finish.

My knees went weak. I slumped to the kitchen floor beside the sink, sobbing with my head in my hands. Body-heaving, shoulder-rolling, gut-wrenching, sickening, gasping sobs. Anne-Marie. My tree. All I had.

I'd already lost everything I used to have back in Meadow Springs: Dorothy, my grandparents, aunts and uncles and all my cousins. All I had. He wanted to take it all away.

I felt Mama's hand below my arm, gently lifting me to my feet, walking me up the stairs, stroking my hair. Curled tightly on my unmade bed, head buried in my pillow, I cried. Cried to the crackle of Jessamyn's temper. Cried through Iris's thudding ill-tempoed interpretation of *The Soldier's March*, until the hot tears dissolved into a pulsing, pounding headache.

The air in the room was dry, the temperature climbing. Feeling as though I'd suffocate in these four walls, I threw open the window sash and began to climb into my tree, hoping for a breeze. I stopped. What had he said? He said not to leave the house—was getting in the tree leaving the house? I couldn't risk it. Instead I reached out and caressed the green leaves beside the window.

Nearby, Lazarus chirped, his feet gripping the wire halfway up the cage and poking his beak through the wire gaps. "I know how you feel," I whispered. I snapped off a small leafy branch from my tree, closed the window tightly and unclasped the cage door. Lazarus, his wing no longer bound, soared happily around the room. "Here," I called, "Come look outside." I held the branch in front of the closed window. The tree, thick with greenery, the blue sky stretching beyond sight, the white cotton clouds: all visible beyond the glass. After some coaxing, Lazarus landed on the branch and we gazed at the tree together. "They can't keep us from imagining," I whispered.

My thoughts drifted to Iris. She hadn't come upstairs after her piano lesson. I was grateful, but curious. Mama must have told her not to. Maybe she'd heard about the two girls last night and decided she was through with me. I pictured the same scene that had played out in our kitchen happening in hers with her father demanding she not see me outside of school. Maybe Iris had even told her father we'd be there, but she'd sounded sincere last night. My head hurt too much to figure Iris Westin out.

I placed Lazarus and his branch perch into the cage and fastened the clasp. Standing in front of my feed store calendar, I counted the days. Today was Friday, June 22. Twelve days to Independence Day. Twelve days until I was done with the singing and the horrible masked men. I could live through that. But school was a long way off. I circled Tuesday, September 4, in chalk. More than two whole months until I saw Anne-Marie at school! She wouldn't know what was going on for two months! She'd think I decided not to be friends. Would she still want to be my friend after two months? My chest began to hurt along with my head.

I slumped down on the bed, remembering we were supposed to meet at noon today. I'd promised. *A man's only as good as his word.* How I hated that proverb. A person's word didn't mean much when they picked and chose who it applied to. Immigrants, Catholics, and females always seemed to get the short end of the stick. I didn't want to break my promise to Anne-Marie, didn't want to do anything to hurt our friendship, even if we'd only been friends a short time. She wouldn't think much of me if I couldn't keep a promise as small as meeting up at the park.

"Have you done those chores?" Daddy demanded sternly from the stairwell.

"I'm coming." Clumping down the stairs, I asked, "Am I allowed to sit in my tree if I don't go anywhere?"

He nodded. "You may. After those chores are done. It's eleven o'clock and you haven't gathered the eggs yet."

Eleven o'clock! In one hour Anne-Marie would be sitting on the park bench waiting for me, growing more impatient, angry, and disappointed at me by the minute. She'd have to wait two whole months to find out why I didn't show up and by then she'd probably be too mad to ever talk to me again. I had to get word to her. I had to!

As I walked out of the chicken coop with five brown speckled eggs in my basket, I heard the gate creak as Samuel wheeled his red wagon into the backyard.

"I had a delivery on your street. It's not your day, but I thought I'd see if you had laundry to pick up."

Something genius struck my brain. "Are you going by the park?" I asked. He nodded. "Would you do a favor for me?" Something on his face told me he wasn't interested in doing any more jobs for the Hopkins family, and I couldn't blame him. "It's just handing a note to someone at the park." I said.

Samuel bit his lip. "That's all I gotta do? Just hand someone a note. Who?"

I nodded. "All you have to do is take it to the park at noon and hand it to Anne-Marie Lombardi. She'll be sitting on one of the benches. Dark hair, brown—"

"My wash route don't take me by the park" Samuel said.. Ma depends on me to get to our customers on time. Some get real uppity if I ain't on time. Lady who works at the pharmacy docked Ma a nickel last week—said I was late. And I don't want to run into Mr. . . " He looked down. "Well, you know"

The hot shame of two days ago bloomed red across my face. "I understand," I said. The last thing I wanted to do was get Samuel in any trouble. I'd already let him down once. "I'm sorry about what happened. I should have explained to Deacon Westin. I just, I just got all scared and tongue-tied. I . . ." I licked my dry lips and thought of

Samuel cuddling that skinny orange cat he loved. "I should have done more." Samuel looked up, studying my face. "I'll go get the wash," I said. "Forget the note. I don't want to get you in any trouble."

Samuel pulled the piece of paper on which he'd written all the day's accounts from his pocket. He tore a scrap from it and pulled a stub of pencil from behind his ear. "I'll get her the note."

Relief washed over me. Relief that Samuel didn't hate me and Anne-Marie would know I wasn't ignoring her. The note had to be innocent, something no one else would understand if it ended up in the wrong hands.

School work is giving me trouble.

Big problem. Can't make it out.

I handed him the note and went upstairs to get the wash. Mama only had a small bundle of clothes tied in a sheet. With each step back down the stairs, daddy's words rolled around in my head. Forbidden to see her. Take an axe to that tree. A man's only as good as his word.

Samuel placed the clothes in his wagon.

"Can I have the note back?" I asked, before pulling two apples from my pocket. I handed one to Samuel and bit into the other as I looked at the ragged scrap, fighting back an urge to tear it to pieces. Then, I took a deep breath, squeezed my eyes shut, and sent up a little prayer to God and all his angels. If you're listening up there, I'm about to break two commandments, but only because I want to make things right. With a shaky hand, I added a third line.

Will try to add a week and 12 hours to the number we agreed on.

I handed him back the note along with a nickel from my birthday money. "For taking up extra time," I explained. As Samuel passed the planter ledge, he looked down at the nickel in his palm, then turned back and looked at me before placing it on the planter ledge. "Keep it." I followed him to the gate to give it back, but Samuel wouldn't take it. I owed him double now, for my not speaking up and for his doing me a favor. As the gate creaked closed behind his red wagon piled high with laundry bundles, I realized I didn't owe Samuel a debt. I'd been given a gift, the gift of his friendship. And I was grateful.

CHAPTER 18

SCREAMING

Being good is hard. And boring. But after my father's threat to cut down my tree, I played the part very well. I dusted every surface in sight, practiced my song whenever my father was in hearing range, and washed dishes after every meal. I played the part of obedient, well-dressed and well-mannered minister's daughter so well I almost believed it myself. I thought the better I acted, the better my chances that my father might forget what he said about chopping down my tree. But the good girl act was only a cover for the bad girl who was a bundle of nerves waiting and plotting to meet up with Anne-Marie.

When you're anxious about something you have to do, the waiting is way worse than the actual doing. Getting a tooth pulled isn't nearly as bad as listening to the grinding drill from the waiting room. When the day arrived for me to meet Anne-Marie by cover of darkness, waiting until midnight was nearly impossible. Every chime of the parlor clock made me waver in my conviction: risk it or play it safe?

While dusting the parlor I was confident I'd do it. Sweeping the floors, I lost my nerve. Mopping, I renewed my vow while swirling soapy water on the linoleum. Over salad at dinner I changed my mind. By the custard dessert I'd changed it back. The whole dinner was tasteless. The dishwater on my hands afterward tepid. Hours on hours piled up. At sunset I went out to visit the chickens. I petted docile Olive's soft red feathers as she sat on her straw nest. Fed Dorothy a scrap of green apple peel from my pocket, then scattered more peels on the straw around the nesting boxes. Jessamyn charged from the open coop yard through the door connecting it to the nest boxes and gobbled up the treats before her sisters could demand a share.

Backing away, I quietly closed the door, locking her in the nesting area. No one was coming out to squawk at me tonight.

Like a fraud, I came downstairs in my blue summer nightgown at 9:30 to tell my parents goodnight. Then I fed Lazarus a little apple peel I'd saved and covered his cage lightly with my apron before lying in bed waiting for my father's feet on the stairs. Ten o'clock chimed quietly downstairs. Ten-thirty. Ten forty-five. At 11:00 he peeked in, the stairwell light glowing behind him. I feigned sleep until he closed the door then lay awake staring at the ceiling, waiting.

I waited for the half hour chime, then the one I'd been expecting. At 11:45 I snuck out of bed and slipped into the clothes I'd hidden at the bottom of the wardrobe, a worn pair of overalls, nearly too small for me, a torn, dark flannel shirt of Daddy's I'd picked from the rag bin, and an old black felt hat. I hoped the dark colors would blend in with the night and if Dr. Arnell or anyone else saw me they'd think I was a boy. With a hairpin I fastened my braids up under the cap and stood by the open window. Was it worth it? Worth risking the tree? Worth breaking my father's trust again? Given his recent better mood, I could have asked if I could visit Anne-Marie. Could have maybe done it in daylight, but I feared his answer would still be no and the question would just land me back in trouble. That was no excuse for what I was about to do, and I knew it. Still, I had to do this one thing. Just this one thing. I owed it to Anne-Marie to explain why I had to sing, to ask her to understand what I had to do it. Did doing a bad thing to do a good thing make it an even swap?

I swung myself out of the window before I could change my mind, looked heavenward and prayed, "Sorry. I swear I'm trying to do the right thing for my friend. You know, the one you sent me when you answered my prayer?" As I shimmied silently down the trunk, I added, "Thanks for that, by the way."

The house was dark. The chickens quiet in their nesting area as I crept by. Even the gate cooperated, sliding open soundlessly. Darkness hugged me close, casting a quarter slice of moon in the indigo sky above to guide me as I snuck past slumbering houses and silent shops to the park.

Weaving through the benches, I chose a big tree next to the pergola to hide behind. I crouched low beside its base, where no one would see me, and waited for my friend's approach. Minutes passed. Had she understood the cryptic message? Had Dr. Arnell been to her house and gotten her grounded, too? Or maybe she was back in Muncie again. Maybe she couldn't sneak out.

In the distance something moved. I couldn't make it out, but by its height I knew it was a person. Along the sidewalk, now crossing toward the park. I held my breath. The figure grew closer then stopped near the benches. I couldn't see the face, but I had to risk it. "Over here," I whispered.

She walked toward the sound of my voice. I reached out to touch her shoulder. "Someone saw us the other night. The man in front of the office was Dr. Arnell. Did he tell your family?" I asked.

She shook her head. "No, he wouldn't risk his Protestant soul being seen at the house of a Catholic." She laughed. "Probably afraid we'd try to convert him and make him pray to a saint or something."

"What about you?" I asked. "Did you get home before your family noticed you were gone?"

"It all worked out. Mama and my grandparents went to her friend's house to celebrate afterward."

That was a relief. Like I'd figured, Dr. Arnell wouldn't be caught dead at Lombardi's Feed, even to tell on Mrs. Lombardi's daughter. "Listen," I said. "I'm in serious trouble. I can't see you until school starts. Punishment for sneaking out that night."

Anne-Marie sucked in her breath. "I didn't mean to get you in any trouble."

"It's okay. I just didn't want you thinking for the rest of summer I wasn't your friend anymore." I paused. "Maybe by September it'll all blow over. That okay? Still friends?"

In the dark I saw her head bob up and down. "Always friends. I didn't think you'd come, new girl. Thought you'd be like all the others."

I winced, hoping she couldn't see me in the dark. "I have to tell you something," I said.

A pair of headlights turned onto the town square. I pulled Anne-Marie against the cover of the tree. The truck rounded the town square slowly, its headlights sweeping along the street before turning back the way it came.

"That truck just about scared me to death," Anne-Marie squeezed my hand. "We better get going."

"Wait. I gotta be honest with you." Talking to her about it was easier in the dark since I couldn't see the disappointment I knew my words would bring. "I tried to get out of that singing, but I have to do it. Not because I want to." I kicked the grass with my toe. "Because my father and Mr. Westin are going to have it in for me if I don't. Please don't be mad at me."

Anne-Marie's silence was shattered by a distant noise. Voices whooping and hollering. The volume growing louder, closer, angrier, coming at us. "Run!" she screamed and pushed me away.

She ran toward the feed store, disappearing from view, swallowed in the darkness. I sprinted across the street, my foot hitting the sidewalk pavement just as the headlights swept around the corner, barreling toward me. I dove behind the wooden Indian standing guard at Holland's store. Peeking from behind the shelter of his carved arm, I saw the back of the pickup was now filled with white-hooded men. Angry and agitated, their hate-filled slurs and obscenities slashed the night's once gentle slumber.

When they passed, I stepped out, terrified to see whether Anne-Marie had made it home. The truck stopped forty yards ahead of me. I scooted back toward the wooden statue. One man stood, raised a Mason jar in a toast, then lifted the bottom of his hood and drank. Had to be alcohol judging by the sounds of their cheering. The nerve of them smashing that still in the newspaper story. What hypocrisy!

Suddenly, a flame illuminated the dark sky above the truck bed, then another. Two blazing bottles spotlighted their evil hooded heads swaying with laughter and vile screams.

"Time for the fireworks show, boys!" one of them yelled as the first bottle sailed through the feed store window, shattering the glass. "That's music to my ears!" Another shouted as together they laughed, and jeered. The store's interior burst aglow as the tongues of flame licked greedily at the maroon curtains.

"No!" My scream, pitiful and powerless, drowned among a sea of triumphant cheering.

"Go home you damn foreigners!" The second bottle skittered across the sky, grazing the side of the building and landing behind the gate where Mr. Lombardi kept the livestock. A huge spiraling blaze sprung up in the dry straw, its orange tendrils grabbing at the metal gate slats. A terrible screeching erupted, screaming, keening, unhuman wailing. And still the noise of hate and alcohol filled men. They clapped one another on the back and raised their fists in the air.

Suddenly, quick as it had come, the truck lurched, sending its tipsy occupants laughing and swaying, and sped away. The laughter and victory shouts faded. As fast as my feet would carry me, I ran to the feed store screaming, "Fire! Fire!" at the top of my lungs. Screams poured from Lombardis' pulverized window. Horrible, unearthly cries rose from the side yard, prickling the hair on the back of my neck.

Anne-Marie tore through the street from her hiding place. "Mama! Grandma!" The screeching nearly drowned her out.

No! No God, not the Lombardis. I jumped through the broken window, sliding on pebbles of glass and grabbed an empty oat bag to beat the flames climbing the curtain. Mr. Lombardi yanked the fiery drapes, rod and all, from the wall, throwing them out the open window before stamping on the blaze. Mrs. Lombardi rushed past me, throwing a pitcher of water on the curtains. The fire grew in strength, the smoke making it hard to see and to breathe. Horrible minutes passed as we doused the flames, beat the flames, even stamped on the flames as they reignited. The screeching penetrated my ears as Mrs. Lombardi and I beat at the fire while Anne-Marie and her grandmother ran up and down the stairs with pitchers of water.

When the curtain fire was quenched, Anne-Marie sat down on the blackened linoleum and sobbed in her grandmother's arms. The inside flames subsiding, Mr. Lombardi turned his attention to the gate outside. Anne-Marie's mother carried water outside to him. Finally, the flames reduced to an amber glow. The eerie shrieking subsided, then stopped. A terrible stench filled the air, smoke, singe and something far worse.

Mrs. Lombardi returned, collapsing next to her mother-in-law and wrapping her arms around Anne-Marie. Mr. Lombardi followed. His hair and mustache were singed, his nightshirt tattered with black, brittle burn marks. He held two bedraggled chickens in his red, soot-streaked arms. I gasped. The inhuman screeching. Mama's ten chickens.

He checked on his family, then placed the two chickens in a wire cage in the back of his truck. I stood frozen and numb, watching the elderly gray-haired Mrs. Lombardi's long, loose braid sway as she rocked her sobbing granddaughter and daughter-in-law on the scorched floor. Mr. Lombardi returned, pried the burned burlap feed bag from my hands and gently brushed soot from my hot cheek. "Go home, little one." He kissed the top of my head. "I thank the angels for putting you two girls in the right place tonight."

CHAPTER 19

A LOUD SILENCE

How loud can one little town's silence be? As I walked home, dazed and dumb, I suddenly stopped in front of Holland's carved statue, feeling something was wrong. Glancing around, I saw no trucks, no white hooded men. But wrong hung heavy in the night air, icy and unwelcome as a splash of well water in the dead of winter. I shook my head, telling myself no one was watching me, unlike the other day when I visited. I could see no lights in shops, no faces peering from behind windows. No one standing on the pavement. I trudged on. As I rounded the corner toward my house it struck me. I turned back to look again down the town square.

No one had come to help. No bucket brigade. No fire truck. No neighbors wrapping the Lombardis in comfort and blankets. No one answered my cries of fire. No one. Other than a puff of white smoke in the distance, it was as though it never happened. The night had already snuffed it out, and the neighbors, content it had cost them only sleep, had kept quiet and already swept it from their consciences.

No one in Grayson Indiana that night cared that my best friend and her family came close to death. As I climbed the tree to my room, a horrible thought crept into the smoke-charred chamber of my brain. Had Daddy been with them? I slipped, clawing at the bark to regain my hold. No. I didn't believe it. Wouldn't believe it. Still, bitter bile rose in my throat.

Too weary to move, too trapped in thought to sleep, I stayed in my tree until dawn's first light washed over the horizon. Nightgown in hand, I crept into the bathroom and filled the basin with cool water. My face and arms were smudged with gray soot. My hat had fallen off sometime in the night and one braid pinned to my head had a singed spot, like a black bruise against my ginger hair. My hair and clothes smelled of smoke, but I avoided the bathtub as the pipes would make too much noise. With a washcloth, I rinsed soot and smoke from my face and body, unpinned my hair and ran a wet comb through it. Burned strands fell to the floor in a damp clump. I sighed and rebraided it so no one would notice the missing hair.

I stuffed my smoky clothes in my school bag, planning to give them to Samuel on his next trip so Mama wouldn't question the smell. Finally, though my room was bathed in dappled morning sun, I crawled into bed and slept.

It seemed like only minutes passed before Mama stuck her head in the door. "I've been calling you."

Swinging my tired, heavy feet from the bed, I slipped into a purple dress, tied my apron behind my back, and started downstairs. Odd. To sleep and dress and descend stairs like every other day even though the whole world had changed overnight.

Plopping down, heavy and sleepy, I sat at the table to await breakfast. Mama wrinkled her brow. "Breakfast was two hours ago. I let you sleep." She felt my forehead. "Seems like you needed it. Are you feeling bad?"

"Just tired."

"If you bring in the eggs, I'll scramble you one," Mama offered.

Shaking my tired, achy head, I grabbed the gathering basket. "No, thanks."

Opening the door between the chicken yard and the nesting boxes, I got a peck from Jessamyn for my trouble. "Be glad you weren't back at the feed store last night." I grabbed the flapping bird, held her tight and sobbed in her snowy feathers until she wriggled away. Tilting back to sit on my heels, I looked at Dorothy, Olive and the others, wondering if I'd ever be free of the screeching in my head.

Tears spent, I gathered the eggs, but dropped one when voices at the gate startled me. The yoke landed sunny side up atop my shoe, the gooey clear fluid spreading out over my toes. Stamping the goo off in the straw, I watched Mr. Lombardi follow Mama into the back yard. His sleeves were rolled up and both arms were bandaged. A spot of blood had seeped through below his right elbow. He carried last night's wire cage holding the two Leghorn survivors from last night, their feathers scorched and dusted with soot. One had a bandage around her neck, much like the shopkeeper's.

I stepped out of the coop and stared at him as he talked to Mama. "She told me to tell you their names are Thelma and Violet, but I do not remember who is which." He put the cage down and our eyes met. Before I could open my mouth, he hurried on, addressing me. "Ah, you wonder about the bandages? I am fine. There was a fire, but we are all well. Anne-Marie is well."

Tired and drained, I stood speechless. There was a fire? Did he think I'd forgotten? The smoke cleared in my mind for a moment and I realized it was for Mama's benefit. Anne-Marie must have told him how we'd met in secret, how I wasn't supposed to be there. I nodded and smiled. "I'm sorry you were hurt. And glad everyone is okay."

"Thelma and Violet not so okay, but your Mama is going to fix them." He turned to Mama. "Please, Signora, I ask again. You keep the money. You do me a favor by taking them so I do not have to move them."

"No, no, Mr. Lombardi. I'm glad to have them." She folded the old man's fingers over the coins he held out to her.

"What do you mean have to move them?" I asked. "Are you going somewhere?"

Mr. Lombardi nodded. "Muncie. My nephew lives there. We do business together in Muncie, now."

"What about Anne-Marie and her mother? Where will they live?" Even as the words left my lips, I knew the answer, and tears welled in my eyes.

"They come with us." He thanked Mama once more then looked around and asked, "Is the priest home, Signora?"

Mama shook her head. "He's visiting a man who's recently widowed."

"Ah," Mr. Lombardi smiled and pointed at the wire cage. "Please, if Esther could take to my truck for me." He held up his bandaged arms. "Would help me."

Mama nodded. I picked up the cage and followed Mr. Lombardi outside to his truck. Sliding the cage in the truck bed, I started to babble, "I'm going to miss Anne-Marie. Will you tell her? Tell her I'm sorry about the singing. About . . ." The old man looked toward the church, then down the street before holding a finger to his lips to quiet me and reaching in his pocket. He pulled out something silver and shiny. He placed it in my hand. "For you. From Anne-Marie."

The necklace had an oval pendant. A robed man surrounded by the words St. Jude. "Who is St. Jude?" I asked. The old man smiled. "The Baptists no have saints, I forget. He is the patron saint of hope. You remember my nipotina when you wear it, no?"

As the truck pulled away, I slipped the necklace over my head, then tucked it safely beneath my dress, suspecting my father wouldn't be pleased to see me wearing a Catholic medal.

When I'd finished all my chores, I closed the window and door in my room and let Lazarus fly free between the four walls. He looked so happy soaring near the ceiling, which made me all the sadder realizing I had nowhere to fly. Confined to the house until Wednesday. No friend to share the rest of the summer. Not even the start of school to look forward to now. I ran my finger across the chalk circling Tuesday, September 4, and smudged the circle out on the navy calendar. Immediately, I felt guilty, like I'd just smudged Anne-Marie out of my life. My nose tingled and my eyes smarted, but no tears came. All cried out.

I returned Lazarus to his cage and carefully perched the cage on the open window sill before climbing out and reaching for the cage. Now we were both in the tree. Lazarus chirped merrily, clawing and climbing up and down the wire with his scaly feet, his eyes darting at all the sights: trees, chickens, grass and church. Above us another bird chirped a greeting and Lazarus responded, "Wah-wooty-wooty-wooty-woo!" He was more excited than I'd ever seen him. I closed my eyes and swore I'd never do anything to jeopardize this tree again. The tree and Lazarus were all I had now.

There was a knock at my door. Daddy stuck his head inside. "Would you come down, please? Deacon Westin would like to see you." Before I could answer, he was gone. Did he know about last night? Had he seen me? My heart began to race. I almost lost my grip on Lazarus's cage as I climbed through the window. With trembling hands I returned his cage to the bureau top, smoothed my braids down and walked toward the stairs. I reached for my neck, assuring myself the necklace was covered by my dress. Stay calm.

He stood in the parlor with my father, beside the piano. "Good afternoon." He tipped his hat, but the gray eyes beneath his straw brim were cold as day-old dead fish.

"Since the deacon has gone to a lot of trouble arranging the entertainment for Wednesday, he'd like to make sure you're ready." My father smiled coolly, politely. "Of course, I assured him you are, but he's a little nervous after last Thursday's dinner. Told me he'd like to hear you for himself."

I let my breath out. They didn't know. Mama joined me at the piano bench and arranged the sheet music. What if they found out? I closed my eyes and sang as scenes from last night flashed in my memory. Flaming bottles. Burning curtains. Shattered glass.

"I sing because I'm happy. I sing because I'm free. His eye is on the sparrow." My voice caught as last night's noise filled my ears. "And I know he watches me."

Mr. Westin nodded brusquely. "Rehearsal is two o'clock Monday at the Methodist church." He nodded to Mama and me and exited our front door without another word to my father.

Mama and Daddy exchanged looks. For the first time in a long time I saw something in Daddy's eyes. Something I hadn't seen since the days he returned skin-and-bones and all nerves back from the Great War. Not shell-shock. Was it . . . fear in his eyes? For the first time it occurred to me that Daddy may be trying to protect our family. Maybe he was neither oblivious nor a coward.

Closing the music cover, I ran my finger over the picture of the sparrow, thinking of Mama's eight lost chickens, wondering why bad things happened to innocent little birds.

CHAPTER 20

SLIPPING

Strange how you can't get rid of painful memories but can't fully hold on to good ones. The fire was always on my mind. But my memory of Anne-Marie, like my memory of Dorothy, was already slipping away. It had only been three days and the pictures in my mind were blurring at the edges. Sitting in my tree, St. Jude nestled close to my heart, I wished I had a photograph of Anne-Marie. Her smile captured in sepia tones and bordered in a gold frame like the picture of me sitting on Daddy's desk. I think now I understood a little better about Daddy's war memories. Month after month in the trenches, the fear, the smell of death. Daddy never talked about it, but I'd heard my uncle whisper about it.

Up in my sanctuary, I thumbed through the gilt-paged hymnal, searching for words, searching for strength, to get through this rehearsal day. Below me, Mama knelt, serene in her holy place, surrounded by straw and grass, humming as she fed Olive from her outstretched palm. Nuzzling Jessamyn. Soothing Violet and Thelma with sympathetic whispers and soft, gentle strokes. "All is well, sweet hens, all is well." Dear Mama! She never suspected she was comforting a bigger audience than just her hens. Closing my eyes, I let her blessed assurance wash over me.

Even after Mama went inside for Iris's piano lesson, the soothing effect of her calm spirit lingered, lulling her feathered flock as they quietly roamed their grassy pen. Music drifted from the parlor. Notes that strolled together smoothly, rhythmically, to compose a tiny slip of a tune. Real, recognizable music! Iris was falling under Mama's spell, too.

When the last piano note faded away, I climbed back into my room. When I heard the knock on my door, I'll admit I wasn't unhappy to see Iris. She sat on the corner of my bed. "I brought you something." She smiled and handed me a rolled paper tied in green ribbon from her beaded bag.

Hoping that Ida and Lillian weren't missing any of their notes or possessions, I unrolled it and gasped. Lazarus! Holding the drawing beside the bird's cage to compare, I swear I couldn't tell them apart. His sharp, butter-colored beak, plump, curved marmalade breast, fine, intricate russet and bronzed feathers. It was a perfect replica. She'd drawn him sitting on a tree branch, framed by a windowsill. My windowsill. Just as if I were inside my room, looking out the window at Lazarus perched in my tree. My tree! My bird!

I hugged her tightly, surprising both of us. Embarrassed, I stammered, "It's beautiful. It's perfect! It's . . . You're . . . You're such a good artist! Thank you so much!"

Smoothing the paper after our awkward hug, I noticed she had signed it in the bottom right corner. Her perfect, curly school script read

For Esther

Your Friend,

Iris Westin

"I thought it would cheer you up," Iris said.

It was no surprise she'd know Anne-Marie was gone. Her father probably bragged about it at the dinner table. Bet her father did a whole lot of bragging. Bet Iris knew everybody's business in town because of him. A piece of the puzzle I'd been wondering about slid into place. "You knew, didn't you?" I asked. "After dinner that night. You knew what was going to happen didn't you?" I threw the drawing beside her on the bed. "You knew and you didn't warn Anne-Marie."

Iris shook her head. "No. I didn't know, Es." She jumped from the bed and grabbed me by the shoulders. "Esther, I swear I didn't know." Her eyes brimmed with tears. "But, I . . . I knew what could happen." She brushed a well-manicured fingertip beneath her eye. "The kind of thing that always happens." She clutched her fist to her mouth and closed her eyes, trying to stem the flood of tears. "Whatever was going to happen, whenever it was going to happen, I didn't want you to be there. Didn't want it to happen to you."

I didn't have any words stacked at the ready for this. Probably couldn't have gotten them going if I had, because the jumble of feelings whirling in my head would have knocked any ready-made proverbs or smart saying over like a stack of milk bottles at the carnival. Disappointment. Sadness. Anger. But some pictures tumbled around in the mix, too. Mr. Westin spewing his hate at Samuel as I watched wordlessly. I doubt time would ever soften the edges of that shame or blur the sharp stab of pain I felt remembering it. Not to mention remembering what I had done to help, which was nothing. When it came right down to it, I was no better than Iris at standing up for others.

"It's okay," I said, handing her my handkerchief. "I understand."

At 1:45, Mama sent me to the church to collect Daddy. He was walking me to the rehearsal. Probably didn't want me to engage in any activities unbecoming our family along the way. I pulled the heavy wooden church door open. The air inside smelled as dry and brittle as the pages of an ancient, worn book. Summer sun poured through the stained glass windows, dabbing paintbrushfuls of pastel color on the wooden floor. Tiny dust motes danced in the slants of kaleidoscope light.

Kneeling before the altar in prayer, he hadn't heard me. I waited quietly, watching his rolled shoulders and bowed head. Though I couldn't hear his prayer, I felt guilty, like the eavesdropper I was, so I coughed loudly.

He rose from his knees and escorted me out the door. No words passed between us. When we reached the Methodist church, he took my hand and walked me up the steps. Day after tomorrow it would all be over for me, but what about him? I feared he'd become another Deacon Westin and drift further and further from me. We sat on a wooden pew until it was my turn. Under the deacon's watchful eye I sang, just as I'd done for him in our parlor. Words might fail me when I talked, but lyrics never forsook me. As I sang, I closed my eyes, trying to picture a time when I really did sing because I was happy and free. After less than four weeks in this town, the memory of the real me was slipping away, too.

CHAPTER 21

A JOB TO DO

Flag-waving, parade-marching, watermelon-eating, star-spangled Fourth of Julys had always been a day to look forward to. Today was different, though. Despite the fact I was no longer grounded, I wasn't interested in leaving the house for any of it.

Though it was nearly time to leave, I dawdled. Watched Lazarus climb his wire cage wall. The leaves on the branch I'd put in a few days ago were curled and dry, scattered across the cage bottom. He deserved a new, fresh, leafy branch. I plucked one from the tree and carefully closed the window sash before opening Lazarus's cage. He flew around the room twice before his feet clasped the branch I held out. I lifted him to the closed window to look out. He chirped merrily. Wah-wooty-wooty-woot-woo!

Without warning Lazarus launched himself at the closed window, bumping the glass and sliding down to the sill, his feathers askew. I snatched him up, checking to make sure he wasn't hurt. Relieved he was only stunned, I again lifted him to the glass to look out. He struggled to flap his wings under my grip, wanting the tree, the wind, the sky, the freedom.

"You're the only friend I have left," I whispered. His beady black eyes pleaded with me. He struggled again, then relaxed in my hands.

"It's time to go," Daddy called from downstairs.

Time to go. Daddy was right. It was time to go. Before I could change my mind, I pushed the window sash up with one hand, kissed Lazarus atop his head, leaned out the window and opened my palm. "Go, sweet bird. Don't forget me."

With a tiny woot to celebrate his independence, Lazarus launched free. Bronzed feathers glinting in the sun, flapping in joy, he soared the blue sky past the coop, beyond the church steeple and out of my sight.

"Did you hear me?" Daddy asked as he entered my room. "It's time."

I suppressed a scream. He had a white robe folded over his arm. Smiling. My own father. I'd hoped, I'd prayed, I'd fooled myself into imagining it would turn out differently. But here he was, my own flesh and blood with a white robe draped over his arm.

"You look nervous," he said. "It's just stage fright. You'll do fine." He reached out to touch my arm, to reassure me, but I pulled away as though the billowing white fabric would burn me if I came in contact with it. I followed him to the stairs, surprised my legs cooperated. "I know you'll make the whole town proud," he said.

He turned around. "Haven't you forgotten something?" Numb, I glanced around me. "I'll get it." He returned from my room and handed it to me. "Your robe."

Crisply starched and smelling of soap and sunshine it could have been mistaken for a baptismal robe. If only we were going down to the river to wash away our sins and rise clean and pure from the water. Not able to bear the thought of wearing it, I draped it over my arm. I mumbled, "I'll put it on later," and silently prayed for a miracle that might allow me not to.

Mama waited for us by the front door. Never one to waste good things extravagantly, she'd worn her mint green dress—last year's second best. She held an apple pie in hand and worry etched on her forehead. Violet wasn't eating. The burn on her neck had become infected and I knew Mama feared she'd lose another of her girls. Daddy plucked a singed feather from her sleeve as we walked out the door.

As we joined the swell of people on Main Street, I felt lonelier than ever among them. Smiling, happy families chattered as they headed, picnic baskets and folded blankets swinging on their arms, toward the park in the center of the town square. Alongside them, children rode bicycles and waved miniature flags, others pulled wagons draped in red, white and blue bunting. The bells above the grocer, tobacconist, and baker's stores jingled merrily as customers shopped for last minute supplies. The whole street pulsed with anticipation for the Independence Day picnic and parade. Even the weather, with its royal blue sky and buttercream clouds, was dressed to celebrate.

The warm summer sun may have swept Friday night's dark horrors from the street with a whistle and a wink, but I still remembered. The braids I had pinned up were still singed. I still smelled the smoke and burning flesh in my memories. Still tasted the dry, acrid burn against the back of my throat. The keening of trapped, burning chickens as they died in terror lived on in my head. The statue knew, too. His walnut brown carved wooden eyes had seen it all as he stood guard at the tobacconist's door and sheltered me from the angry, alcohol-fueled men. Men, who with five days sobriety under their belts, now shepherded their laughing families alongside us toward the park.

There'd be no hiding from them now. I trudged along staring at the pavement, until I heard Mama gasp. I looked up. Lombardi's Feed was mere yards away. Its soot-stained bricks bore witness to the terror inflicted on its occupants. Scorched tatters hung from the metal skeleton that had once been a window awning. Someone had painted a message on the plywood boards nailed over the broken window.

THIS CITY CLEAN-UP PROJECT

BROUGHT TO YOU COURTESY OF

THE INVISIBLE EMPIRE

I stared at the feed store, refusing to be nudged along by my father. I would see it and so would he, whether he liked it or not. Blood surged through my body. Pulsing, pounding, rising hot and steady.

Trash. That's what Westin and his gang thought the Lombardis were. Trash to be burned up, swept away and tossed out.

I spun around to face my father. "Do you see that? Do you see what they did?"

Mama nodded toward the sign. "Do you think the fire was intentional? Someone tried to hurt the Lombardis? The animals?" Daddy shook his head, unwilling to see the plain truth.

"Of course they did it on purpose!" I slapped my palm against his chest. I wanted to scream, but Daddy's tight-lipped expression warned me to hold it in.

Daddy dropped the picnic basket and stood frozen, staring at the burned hull of Lombardi's Feed. He didn't even try to move my hands, now clinging to the front of his shirt. "We can't be so quick to judge." But his voice was wooden. His eyes dull. "Can't assume. Don't know for certain who this Invisible Empire is."

"I do know!" I clutched his shirt tighter. "I saw it happen."

"You what?" He knelt down on one knee to look in my eyes. "How could you have seen this, Esther Grace?"

I bit my lip. My tree. The last friend I had. What if he followed through on his threat to chop it down? But he had to hear what he'd gotten himself into, even if it cost me everything dear. "I snuck out Friday night." Before he could interrupt I insisted, "Listen! I had to apologize to Anne-Marie. Tell her I couldn't see her anymore. We met at the park at midnight. When I was leaving. That's when it happened." I pointed to the wooden Indian statue. "I hid there. A truck load of men in white robes and hoods did it. They lit bottles and threw them through the window and over his fence. Afterward I ran to help. My hair got burned." A tear rolled down my face. I pushed it away. "The chickens. Oh, Mama, I heard the chickens."

I fell against Daddy's chest and cried. He stood still a long time, stroking my hair. "She could have been killed, Paul," Mama said. "You've seen the chickens, what's left of them. The Lombardis all could have been killed.

My tears had soaked a wet spot into Daddy's shirt. I clutched a handful of it once more and looked up at him. "Don't put that robe on. Please, Daddy. You're not one of them."

My father clasped his hands over mine and a shadow of a fear flashed across his eyes. He licked his lips nervously. Did he finally see the truth, or was he finally willing to admit it? Hope flickered inside me. Seeing the feed store, hearing the truth, it had convinced him. I smiled back. He stroked my hair, unpinned my braid and ran a finger along the frizzled black burned ends I'd tried to hide. "We can talk this all over later, but right now you need to keep your word and sing." He held up a finger to quiet my protest. "I know it's hard, but you have a job to do." He looked me in the eye. "For your family."

CHAPTER 22

THE COSTUME

A costume. That's what my father called it. "Get in your costume and find your place." Like this was all a play and the white robes were as innocent as the gnome hats and fairy wings hanging on racks in the back of the school auditorium. But this was no fairy tale.

He steered Mama by the elbow toward a bench at the park. I wanted to run. Hide. I looked back at Lombardi's Feed. What if we were next? If I didn't do what they wanted, what would happen? It could be our parlor window. Our curtains on fire. My parents stamping out flames. Our family run out of town.

Pinning my hair back in place, I found my spot with the other singers under the shade of an oak tree beside the stage. I'd waited for Anne-Marie in this very spot on that dark night. The crowd gathered on benches and blankets spread on the grass. I knew some of them had been here Friday as well. Still others had waited behind the safety of their window shutters, their silence painting them just as guilty.

Iris took the stage to recite the Preamble to the Constitution. "We the people of the United States, in Order to form a more perfect Union, establish Justice, insure domestic Tranquility, provide for the common defence, promote the general Welfare . . ."

I closed my eyes and remembered Mrs. Lombardi's triumphant speech at the school board meeting a few days ago. She had spoken out so bravely and saved her job. Oh to be as courageous and bold as Mrs. Civilla Lombardi! My stomach lurched remembering how she and her family had been repaid in wrath and revenge.

The choir mounted the steps to sing. I waited, next in line. Dreading the moment. I lifted my eyes heavenward and got straight to the point with God or his spirit or whatever was up there, whispering "Help!"

Above me in the tree something stirred. A flash of bronze glinted in the sun above a marmalade chest. A buttery yellow beak called down to me, "Woot!"

Warm, comforting lyrics washed over me. His eye is on the sparrow, and I know he watches me.

"Esther!" Mr. Westin waved me forward. "You're up next." I stepped toward him. Smelled the peppermint on his breath. Felt the body heat emanating from his robe in the July temperature. He pointed at my arm. "The robe. Put the robe on," he demanded.

From high above, another "Woot!" I shook my head, my eyes pleading with Deacon Westin for mercy. He grabbed my arm, tight as a vice. "I said put that robe on, girl," he hissed in my ear and pressed his thumbs deeper into my flesh sending a jolt of pain toward my neck. "Now!" He pushed my arm away, snatched the folded robe from the crook of my other arm and held it out.

Over his shoulder, I watched a scorched tatter of Lombardi's awning sway in the breeze, warning me. I lowered the zipper, stepped into the robe and zipped it up to my neck with trembling fingers.

"After this last chorus," Mr. Westin demanded.

The robe smothered me. The heat unbearable. I tugged the zipper to loosen it from around my neck, its metal zipper pull hot against my hidden St. Jude medal.

"Now!" He propelled me forward with a push.

I mounted the stage, legs wobbly, arms numb. The old church organist sat at the piano staring at me for a cue to begin. I licked my lips. Must be forty of them sitting in front of me. Men in white robes, hoods pocketed in the midday sun, children and wives smiling and leaning against their arms. Mr. Holland. Dr. Arnell. The principal. Daddy sat among them, a swath of white fabric resting across his lap.

The woman at the piano coughed. Without thinking I turned to look at her. She took it as a signal and began playing. Still, I stood, motionless, missing my cue. The audience began to murmur. The pianist stopped.

Mr. Westin jumped up to the stage, solicitous and syrupy, "Little lady has a case of stage fright. Let's make her feel at home." He clapped and the audience followed. A small boy sitting in his red wagon waved his miniature flag at me enthusiastically. His wagon was new and shiny, and I'd bet my birthday nickel his wheels didn't creak like Samuel's. Samuel, my friend, who wouldn't be welcome at this "patriotic" event. Remembering how I'd let Samuel down, remembering how he'd looked at me like I was a monster when he picked up the robe pattern, remembering all the words I didn't say, I reached for the medal around my neck. Under my breath I whispered, "Help me do the right thing this time."

"Now then," Mr. Westin patted my back gentle as the brush of a butterfly wing, "Let's try that again, sweetheart." He nodded to the pianist.

At that moment, a gust of wind, hot and dusty, whooshed through the park, blowing piano music to the ground, turning picnic blanket corners, scattering straw hats and whistling through the leafy park trees, who lifted their light, breathy voices together in a lilting chorus, whispering to me, lending me their inner strength, strength that had withstood a thousand storms, impelling me to stand tall.

In the stir to gather pages and right picnic baskets, I untied the cord belted at my waist, unzipped the robe and let the cotton yardage puddle at my feet. "I won't sing in that."

Mr. Westin's eyes pierced right through me. I was in for it and I knew it. He turned, smiling, to the audience. Shrugging and turning his palms up in a comical gesture he laughed. "Looks like we got ourselves a temperamental one, folks. One of them big city stage stars!" Laughter rolled across the park. "Guess that robe was too hot, huh?" He plucked his robe out in front of himself with one hand and fanned his other hand over it. "It's true these robes have seen their share of scorching, heat, haven't they boys?" More laughter.

Anger coursed through my veins, heating the words I'd stacked at the ready like firewood. A tiny "Woot!" flew from the oak above and sparked my flame. It fanned my courage until all the tinder piled inside me ignited in an inferno, a raging firestorm I could no longer contain, no matter what the cost. "They're hateful, these robes." I stepped out of the puddle and kicked it away as I pointed toward the feed store. "What people do in them is hateful. I won't be part of it."

A sea of startled faces. Gasps. Mr. Westin stormed to me, snatched both my arms in iron fists and yanked me off the stage. I fell beneath his grip, landing on my knees as he dragged me, knees thumping down the two rough wooden stage steps. He shoved me aside. As I tumbled to the grass, my St. Jude necklace slipped from my neck, and my shoulder popped, shooting pain down my left side. I tried to stand, clutching my shoulder, blood trickling down both knees, gasping in pain, as I scanned the grass in vain searching for St. Jude, my only link to Anne-Marie.

The audience was suddenly alive, people standing, whispering, and pointing. Mama and Daddy rushed forward. Mama ducked beneath my good arm to support me and propped me upright.

Daddy bolted past me toward the stage where Mr. Westin was attempting to get the choir started on another song. He leapt over the wooden stairs stained with a fresh, rusty streak of my blood, strode across the stage and grabbed the head deacon of his church by the arm. All six feet of my father spun him clear around like a toy top so they were face to face.

"You keep your hands off my daughter." He spit the words in Deacon Westin's stunned face. "I'd have the law on you," he clutched the deacon's robe and pointed to the men in the audience. "if there were any law in this town." Reverend Daddy shoved him aside, then wadded up the robe he'd been holding and threw it in Deacon

Westin's face, shouting, "And you can have this godforsaken thing back!"

CHAPTER 23

STUBBORN LIKE THAT

Dear Lord, what had I done? I panicked all the way home, fighting back tears and gulping down the urge to cry in pain as I hobbled up our porch steps, leaning against Mama and Daddy. What was going to happen to us? What trouble had I gotten us into? Were they coming for us now?

As Mama plumped up my pillows and Daddy helped me onto my bed, the doorbell rang. For the rest of the day, it rang and rang, never seeming to stop. Angry voices floated up through the ceiling. Mama, looking worried, peeked in every half hour with fresh ice for my shoulder, or a glass of lemonade or aspirin. Mostly just to fuss over me like I was a baby chick.

What was going to happen to us? Trucks filled with hooded men? Flaming bottles? More burning chickens? Worse? A few hours ago I worried my father might take an ax to my tree. After what I'd done, I worried far worse things were going to happen to my tree, my house, my family. I looked out at my beautiful oak. It was all I had now, and despite my sore shoulder and scraped knees, I gingerly climbed out the window and settled in the arms of the only friend I had left as the sun crept low on the horizon.

I watched Mama scatter feed in the chicken pen. Heard her whisper her thanks as Violet nibbled a bit of watermelon from her hand. I smiled, grateful for a little good news. And as Mama went into the house and began to play the piano, soft as a whispered prayer, I pulled the hymnal from its secret place to follow along. Then I heard a cough. A small, polite, ladylike "excuse-me" sort of cough. Iris Westin stood below my tree looking up at me.

She reached into her beaded bag and pulled something out. "Catch," she whispered, tossing it up to me. I caught the silver chain between my fingers and marveled at the fact Iris Westin had snuck into our back yard and risked her father's wrath for me.

"I thought you'd want it back. To . . ." She shrugged. "To remember her. She used to wear it at school."

As I hung St. Jude around my neck, Iris glanced nervously at our back door and whispered, "I have to go."

"Wait," I said as she turned to leave. "Thank you. For returning it to me. And . . . for being my friend."

Even though I only saw the back of her dress slipping silently out the gate I'd oiled a few days earlier, I knew Iris Westin was smiling. One of her real smiles.

I heard a knock at my bedroom door, then saw my father walk into my empty room. He stuck his head out the window. "Come inside, please. I want to talk to you."

I was proud of him for giving back that robe—even though he'd been given one, proud of him for standing up to Deacon Westin, but I was still angry that he'd gone along with them to begin with. The newspaper, the school board meeting, the fire. All the signs were there, but he had blindly refused to pay attention, to stand up for what was right.

I shook my head. "I don't want to talk." I stared at the sun sinking below the church steeple as silence hung between us.

He sighed. "Well, if you're not coming down, then it goes to reason I have to come up." He took off his shoes and rolled up his sleeves and pant legs. Seeing him sitting on my window ledge, with his long legs dangling down, I almost gave in and told him I'd come inside. Almost. I was stubborn like that. "Hope I can still do this," he muttered.

He reached for the branch next to mine, swung his legs onto it and crawled expertly down the limb until he sat nearby against the trunk.

Where had my father learned to do that? The question must have shone in my eyes or slipped out of my wide-open mouth because Daddy smiled and answered. "I had a tree once, too. I'd sit and read for hours." He pointed at the pilfered hymnal in my lap. "I preferred Jules Verne. *Twenty-Thousand Leagues under the Sea*! My father didn't approve, especially when the cows needed milking."

Questions crowded my mind, but I stubbornly didn't allow any to slip between my tightly sealed lips. Like I had said, I didn't want to talk. Plucking leaves from the tree, I watched them drift down as I wondered what was going to happen to us. Would we survive whatever was coming? Would Iris Westin warn me beforehand? All my questions lay scattered below. Unasked. Unanswered.

The distance between us was less than half an arm's length, but neither of us moved. A warm breeze rippled through the leaves. Daddy sat quietly, patiently waiting, as darkness, like the silence, crept through the branches, ushering in sunset.

"I had to," I finally whispered.

Daddy let out a deep, slow breath. He was quiet for a long time. "You had to sneak out and almost get yourself killed?" He reached for a branch above me to hold as he turned to look me in the eyes. "Or do you mean you had to tell off the whole town and almost get yourself killed?"

I met his gaze straight on. "Both," I said, picking another leaf and sending it sailing toward the shadowy ground below. "Are you really going to chop my tree down?"

Daddy picked a leaf and looked at it. "I bet this fine old oak has seen over a hundred years. It would be a shame to cut it down because of one stubborn little girl." He tossed the leaf in my lap and winked at me. "One stubborn, brave, kind-hearted, very disobedient girl."

"You wouldn't listen to me." I picked up the leaf my father had tossed at me and tossed it back toward him. "You didn't want to hear the truth."

Again he sat quietly, counting, thinking, I wasn't sure. Then he nodded and wiped his eyes with his hand. "I suspected, but I thought I could do some good here. I was wrong." He tossed the leaf back before running his hand along the tree bark. "It would be a shame to cut this tree down because of one pig-headed preacher, too."

My eyes filled again with tears, but not because of my shoulder. I brushed them away. "I heard voices downstairs. Angry voices."

"Oh, yes. Lots of people with lots of things to say," Daddy said.

"Are they mad at us?" I whispered.

"Some of them." Daddy reached in his pocket for a handkerchief. "But some of them are proud. Proud of you, Esther Grace." He wiped his eyes again and handed the handkerchief to me. "Just like I'm proud of you." He smiled. "And they're hoping it means the end to all this hundred percent nonsense."

"What's going to happen now?" I asked.

"I don't know."

"Are they going to fire you from your preaching job?"

"I'm not sure. If they do, there's always potatoes to farm."

"If they don't, are we going to stay here?"

Daddy was quiet for a moment. "That's the question, isn't it?"

I handed him back the handkerchief. Daddy wrinkled his brow, catching sight of the silver St. Jude medal around my neck. He lifted it to get a closer look. "Where did you get this?"

"Anne-Marie gave it to me. It's the apostle Jude, the patron saint of hope."

Reverend Daddy brushed a strand of my burned hair away from my cheek. "It's beautiful. You should wear it proudly. And Muncie isn't that far away, you know. We could visit."

I smiled. "And Mama can get more chickens when we visit."

He clasped my hand from across the branch. His rough, calloused farmer hand was warm and safe. We sat linked in the still, quiet darkness.

An explosion detonated nearby. Daddy flinched and a scream strangled in my throat as I yanked my hand back to cling to the tree trunk. They'd come. The Klan. Deacon Westin. Just like at the Lombardis. Of course they would. I'd known they would. It was all my fault! I scanned the dark yard below for white hoods and flames.

But there were none.

"There," Daddy said, and pointed up to the night sky. A sparkling red chrysanthemum hung above the church steeple for a moment before dissolving in the dark, sacred night.

It was beautiful. I clutched my St. Jude medal, feeling his hope wash over me as a sparkling bouquet of red, white and blue fireworks burst above us.

How had I forgotten? It was Independence Day.

AUTHOR'S NOTE

The early 1920's ushered in many changes in the United States. The Eighteenth Amendment to the Constitution, also known as Prohibition, took effect in 1920, making the manufacture, sale or transportation of liquor a crime. In that same year, women received the right to vote for the first time when the Nineteenth Amendment was passed. Silent movies were still the rage and, with the radio not yet available, many people were only exposed to music at church.

During this time, anti-Catholic and anti-immigrant prejudice was widespread in the United States. Large numbers of white Catholic immigrants, particularly Italian and Irish immigrants, had come to the US in the latter half of the previous century, creating a nativist us-versus-them mentality among some Protestant groups. The Ku Klux Klan, its numbers recently swelled by the 1915 release and 1919 rereleased blockbuster silent movie, *The Birth of a Nation*, claimed Catholics allied themselves to the Pope in Rome and were, thus, not "loyal" Americans. The KKK had been on the decline until the movie's release, but the movie led to the reformation and rebirth of the KKK in 1915. The newly reformed group broadened its hatred and violence toward immigrants and Catholics particularly those coming from Ireland and Italy, during this time, while continuing to target Black citizens.

Klan membership reached its apex in the early 1920s. In Indiana, it was estimated as many as one in three white males claimed membership, including many of those holding government offices. Protestant ministers, like Esther's father, were especially courted by the Klan. They were offered free memberships and robes as well as positions of power within the order in exchange for their public support, and the opportunity to recruit members of their church. It was not uncommon for robed Klan members to appear at a church and present the congregation with a monetary gift.

Some Klan groups campaigned against Catholic business owners by engaging in "clannishness," the practice of doing business only with other Klansmen. Signs proclaiming "100% American," "TWK" (Trade with a Klansman), or "KOTOP" (Klansmen Obey Their Oath Persistently) were posted in Klan-supported shop windows. Businesses were rated at Klan meetings as favorable, neutral or unacceptable. A Klansman seen shopping at unacceptable stores faced the scorn of his peers as well as the possibility of losing his membership, which, under the clannish trade system, might mean losing his livelihood as well.

Those who questioned the Klan's practices or did not heed their warnings faced the possibility of beatings, public cross burnings, or even death at the hands of the Invisible Empire.

ACKNOWLEDGEMENT

The author is grateful to her agent, Amy Thrall Flynn of Aevitas Creative Management, for her help and guidance. In addition, she wants to acknowledge her critique partner, Allison Crotzer Kimmel for her feedback and support.

A big thank you also goes out to Dee Marley for her beautiful cover art.

ABOUT THE AUTHOR

Rebecca Langston-George is the author of nineteen books for children. Her titles have been published internationally and recognized as NCSS-CBS Notable Social Studies Trade Books and appeared on several state reading lists. She received the Armin R. Schultz Award for writing that promotes social justice. A retired educator, Rebecca volunteers as the Regional Advisor for the Society of Children's Book Writers and Illustrators in Central-Coastal California and serves on the board of the California Reading Association. When she's not doing school visits, Rebecca writes and mostly rewrites on a treadmill desk at one mile per hour.

Read more about Rebecca and her books at

www.rebeccalangston-george.com

www.historiumpress.com